~Books by Janice J. Richardson~

Fiction

The Spencer Funeral Home Niagara Cozy Mystery Series

Casket Cache

Winter's Mourning

Grave Mistake

First Call

Nonfiction

The Making of a Funeral Director

(a memoir)

Serve, Protect, & Bury

(a triptych of memoir by front-line workers)

* Amazon * Kobo * Nook * iBooks *

* Chapters/Indigo *

FIRST CALL

A Spencer Funeral Home
Niagara Cozy Mystery

Book 4

Janice J. Richardson

CANADA

ACKNOWLEDGEMENTS

Thank you, Cathy. Without your expertise, this book would not have happened. And thank you MJ and Brian for your professional and valuable editing.

"The purpose of a storyteller is not to tell you how to think, but to give you questions to think upon."

~ **Brandon Sanderson, The Way of Kings**

1

Christmas morning Jennifer felt at loose ends, restless and uneasy, as if something was pending and she couldn't attend to it. She made coffee, and sat on the couch with Grimsby beside her, idly stoking his fur as she pondered her mood. With the funeral home closed and the day ahead of her, she wondered what to do with herself. Taking inventory of her apartment, she decided the laundry needed to be her first chore. If a call came in, she'd get changed and open the funeral home.

Dawdling, Jennifer made herself another coffee, still enjoying her newly-renovated kitchen. But a lingering shadow from events around the renovations plucked at the edges of her mind. Carol, the designer who had remodelled some of the funeral home and her apartment, was still working at her design store.

Two days ago, Jennifer and Marcia had driven by Carol's store after a funeral and noticed Carol's new Audi parked out front. When Jennifer mentioned it to Marcia, she reassured Jennifer that Ryan had not let the matter drop. He and his team were quietly continuing the investigation based on the information Jennifer had discovered late in the case.

Both of them had been silent for the rest of the drive back to the funeral home, their consciences uneasy. Carol may have been able to get away with murder by deflecting the blame to her assistant Agnes. Agnes' death weighed heavily on the two funeral directors. They felt partly responsible for suspecting her of murder. Jennifer had been so caught up in her work and the renovations, she hadn't noticed Agnes' insecurity, mistaking it for indifference. Had her rush to judgement contributed to Agnes' death?

With a tiny sigh, Jennifer put down her now empty coffee cup, picked up her laptop, ignoring the nagging voice in her head telling her to start the laundry, and checked the news.

Coverage continued to focus on the spread of influenza across the country. For the past few weeks, the latest flu outbreak had dominated the news cycle. Jennifer scanned the rest of her favourite news sites, and a few minutes later, closed down her laptop, a sense of foreboding still hanging over her.

FIRST CALL

Holidays were such fun when as a kid. Death wasn't part of the season. Now it seems to be all I think about. Jennifer needed to balance her life better—the fun of getting ready for Marcia's wedding proved that. *Maybe I should go for more walks, at least that lifts my mood.*

Some days, especially Christmas, being an adult wasn't nearly as much fun as being a child. Buying gifts for her staff this year, taking time to choose a present that would suit each person, had also been a reminder to put work behind her once in a while. Jennifer had enjoyed picking out presents she knew each staff member would like.

Elaine, the office manager at Spencer Funeral Home, loved to read; she received a tablet. Jennifer had tucked in a gift certificate for some books to get her started. Peter, her assistant and soon-to-be funeral service apprentice, got a gift certificate to an electronics store. Marcia, her best friend and funeral director was always a challenge to buy for. But Jennifer had finally settled on a gift certificate to the vintage store where they'd bought their outfits for her wedding, and a gift certificate for her favourite shoe store.

Jennifer had fun choosing gifts for the staff at Williams Funeral Home as well. Brent, the manager, got a weekend pass to a resort for his family. Desta, the office manager, and gifted artist, got tickets to an art show in Toronto with an overnight stay at a hotel. To Gordon, her newest hire (a funeral director covering over Christmas), she gave a plane ticket to Ottawa to visit his fiancé later in the week; and Jeff, the assistant, got a gift certificate for a new phone.

Jennifer smiled as she recalled the fun she had shopping for the staff. As a little girl she would dream of being able to give nice presents to her friends. It tickled her to be able to live that dream. She had even bought a present for herself—a red purse. Her other two purses were black and boring. After having worn a red suit and getting her nails done with red polish for Marcia's wedding, she liked the way it made her feel. She decided to move outside her comfort zone more often. Marcia's choice had been correct. Red *was* a good colour for her.

Jennifer had also donated some money to the shelter where Winter had stayed, so the staff and residents could have a Christmas too. Winter was the pregnant young woman Jennifer had found along the Niagara Parkway a few months before. It had given Jennifer great satisfaction to help the girl find her father-in-law, John Wisener. Occasionally thoughts of John would steal her mind, and Jennifer found herself hoping she'd hear from him again. Perhaps he'd let her know when his grandchild was born.

Grimsby, her cat, got a Christmas stocking with new toys and treats and catnip. He kept her entertained Christmas Eve rolling in the catnip, racing up and down and around the apartment until he ran out of steam.

After an uneventful and peaceful few hours cleaning the apartment, the dryer beeped a chirpy reminder her clothes were ready.

"Coming," she said to no one in particular. As she reached for the dryer door another sound clashed with the beeping. It took her a few seconds to realize the discordant noise was her phone, demanding her attention. She covered the few steps to the kitchen island and picked it up, an uneasy feeling that it was probably a first call and her free time was over.

"Spencer Funeral Home, Jennifer speaking."

A familiar pleasant female voice caused her heart to skip a beat. It wasn't a death call.

"Ms. Spencer, Mr. Wisener apologizes for the short notice, but would you be available for dinner this evening?"

"Yes, I would be delighted." Jennifer caught herself smiling as she answered.

"The car will be there at 4:30 p.m. if that is acceptable."

"It is. Thank you very much. Merry Christmas!"

As she disconnected, Jennifer's excitement continued to rise before she realized John was spending his first Christmas without his son, Aaron, who'd died in a skiing accident last winter. She'd met the renowned businessman when he chose Spencer funeral home for Aaron's funeral.

Her feelings for John Wisener were an enigma to her. On the one hand, she had trouble admitting to herself that she had feelings for the reserved and kindly forty-six-year-old businessman; on the other hand, she felt she needed those feelings to go away. Their lifestyles were a dichotomy and she couldn't see how they'd ever meld. *He never once mentioned he had romantic feelings toward me. I'm living in a dream world. He'll be missing Aaron terribly over Christmas and he knows I'll understand. He just doesn't want to be alone, that's all. Neither do you.*

Glancing at the time on her phone, she decided to bake some cookies. She completed the rest of her chores, the smell of baking making her heart lighter than it had been she got up that morning. She took her time filling a couple of festive boxes with the treats and tying them with a bow to take to John and his driver William. But that still left her with the better part of the afternoon before the car's arrival, and excitement at the prospect of an evening out made her restless.

Jennifer called her friend Gwen, on the east coast, to see how her family had spent Christmas. Originally reticent and uneasy about leaving her hometown and moving halfway across the country, Gwen now chattered happily about the weather and the people she'd met since her move, and her kid's new school. Jennifer filled her in about Marcia's wedding and how her twin, Anne, had become good friends with Jim, one of the police officers who'd served as her protection officer after the kidnapping.

"I'm so glad hubby took this job on the coast," said Gwen happily as their call wound down half an hour later. "I miss you and my friends back home, too, but this has been a great adventure for us. I love the ocean. Can't get enough. There's a Tim Horton's at the Wharf and when the kids are in school I get a chai latte and sit and watch the waves."

"I miss our chai lattes together," Jennifer said wistfully.

"I miss our chai lattes together, too. Tim's is open today, go get one, think of the fun we had over the years and toast us."

"I might just do that." As Jennifer disconnected the call, she decided Gwen's idea about the latte was worth the trip out. Grabbing her coat, she went downstairs through the garage to the car. Big fluffy snowflakes tumbled from the sky. She stuck out her tongue and caught one, laughing out loud with delight.

At the drive-thru she said hi to Clair, one of the staff.

"It's busy today," Jennifer said.

"It's always busy over Christmas," Clair responded with her warm smile as she handed Jennifer the latte. Jennifer paid her with a ten-dollar bill and told her to keep the change. "Merry Christmas, Clair."

"You too! See you soon."

The snow had increased, falling faster and thicker by the time she pulled back up to the funeral home. *I'll have to shovel if this keeps up.* Jennifer entered the garage and put the shovel and salt by the door. Just as she hung up her coat, her phone rang. Anne's name and number showed in the display.

She tapped it, and heard her twin say, "Merry Christmas." Jennifer hurried up the stairs, settled on her couch and said, "I half expected you to say this is the obligatory Christmas check-in or something equally sarcastic."

"Naw. It's been great. Jim's here."

A 'hi Jennifer' bellowed from the background. "Hi Jim!" she yelled back, earning a startled glare from Grimsby.

"Sorry, buddy," she said, stroking his fur. He looked at her through slitted and sleepy eyes, not amused by the commotion. "So, what have the two of you been up to besides arguing about the current political climate?"

"We had a great Christmas Eve. Jim took me to the Chateau Laurier for dinner."

Jennifer let out a low whistle. "Wow."

"I know, it was beautiful. After dinner we walked along the canal and watched the skaters and talked."

"What's on your agenda today?"

"We're staying in, I think. I'm making dinner. Tomorrow we may putter around downtown. I managed to wrangle a few days off in spite of the fact the newsroom is short staffed. A couple of people are off with the flu. What have you been up to?"

"So far, having a quiet day. I'm going out for dinner with John tonight. It's been busy the past few weeks. It's my first quiet day in a while. It just started snowing."

"So, Mr. Wisener called you?"

"Not exactly, one of his people did."

"You know what I mean. Is it getting serious?"

Jennifer scrunched up her face, scowling at her twin's comment. "Of course not! It's Christmas. He's probably feeling lonely after losing Aaron. You're reading more into it than what's there."

"Jim and I both think the two of you are meant to be together," Anne said quietly.

"I appreciate the thought, but it's just a friendship. I'm honoured that he wants to spend his holiday with me. It has to be hard on him." She softened her tone. "I'm glad you and Jim are together."

"If you had told me a few weeks ago I'd be in a relationship, I'd have laughed in your face," Anne responded. "I'm not laughing now. It's been wonderful."

"I can tell. You don't seem cranky and detail-oriented. You sound happy. I expect Jim is too."

Jennifer took a breath then asked, "Did you call Mom and Dad?"

Anne sighed deeply. "Not yet. Jim has suggested it twice now, and I will after we hang up."

"In that case, say hi to them for me. I have to run. The funeral home line is ringing. Give Jim a hug for me."

"Will do, catch you later. Merry Christmas!"

The landline was the answering service with a call. They connected Jennifer to the family. A gentleman introduced himself as Mr. Patterson and asked if the funeral homemade arrangements on Christmas Day.

Sensing his urgency, Jennifer agreed to see the family immediately. Glancing at the clock, she gauged her time before she was to go out to dinner. The Patterson family needed support and answers. That was her first priority. If she missed her 4:30 deadline, William would wait and John would surely understand. She changed quickly into a suit then went downstairs. After putting out the coffee supplies in the lounge, she unlocked the door and stood at the entrance, enjoying the snowfall.

She smiled to herself at the thought of Anne and Jim. Anne had vowed she would never settle into a relationship. "Never say never," she said out loud to the falling snow.

Lingering in the chill a little too long, Jennifer slipped back inside and started the file on the call. When the family came in, her mood changed.

As Mr. Patterson introduced himself, his wife and his daughter Victoria, Mrs. Patterson gave way to sobs. Bereavement did not take holidays into account. Christmas would be forever changed for the Patterson family. As Victoria tended to her mother, Jennifer noticed how strained and pale Mr. Patterson looked. Determined to give them all the time and support they needed, she led them to the lounge and offered tea. Victoria helped her get it ready for her parents. Mrs. Patterson continued to sob. Jennifer placed the tea caddy beside the distraught mother and nestled a box of tissues nearby.

Once everyone settled, Jennifer sat back, the silence weighing heavily, and waited until they were ready to speak. When the mother's sobs subsided, she looked up at Jennifer. The anguish in her tear-streaked face tugged at Jennifer's heart.

"We don't know where to start," she said.

"I'm here to guide you. The news of your son's death must have been horrific."

"What do we do now?" asked the father, his fingers tapping on the arm of the chair. "We've never had to deal with this before. The police showed up at our door in the middle of the night. We haven't even been able to see Mike."

"Mike wasn't feeling good last night. I think he was coming down with the flu. He should have stayed home, but he wanted to spend Christmas Eve with his girlfriend. He'd been talking about proposing to her," Mrs. Patterson's voice choked with grief. "We called her this morning. She said Mike had gotten sicker and was wheezing. He didn't have his inhaler with him." She buried her head in her hands and gave into her grief again.

A heavy silence hung over the little group as Mr. Patterson leaned over and gently squeezed his wife's arm.

"So, what do we do now?" Mr. Patterson repeated. He looked into Jennifer's eyes for the first time since the family arrived.

Jennifer spent the next hour doing her best to help them focus on what to expect. She started with the obituary, Mrs. Patterson insisted on it. Unable to focus, she changed the wording over and over. Victoria replaced her mother's forgotten tea as Jennifer excused herself to check with the hospital.

Mike hadn't been released, an autopsy was pending. There was a small backlog, the pathology department had been closed for a few days. The clerk in the admitting department explained she had no timeline for release.

Returning to the lounge, Jennifer sat down and relayed the information. Mr. Patterson was trying to organize the next steps, Mrs. Patterson was still unable to focus and her husband was doing his best not to show his frustration. Victoria had moved closer to her mother, comforting her.

"At this point," said Jennifer quietly, "there's not much that can be done. Once your son is released, I will let you know. It may be a few days. That will give you time to think about what kind of service you want for him and if you still wish to see him. Using the chapel here and holding the reception in the lounge after gives us flexibility. You mentioned your minister was available and will be meeting with you after you leave here?"

Mr. Patterson nodded.

She continued to focus on the father, who clung to every word she said. "I will contact the cemetery, they can arrange to meet with you in the next few days. We have the obituary partially completed, the date and time of the funeral TBA. I'll update it once

Mike is released, and I will call you. Do you want to select a casket now or would you prefer to wait?"

"Now," said the father as the mother said, "Wait." The parents looked at each other, confused by the lack of communication between them.

Victoria broke the silence. "Let's wait, Dad. We have time." The father stared at his wife and daughter, not fully focusing on them. His shoulders sagged as he nodded. He rose, and helped his wife get up. Jennifer walked them to the door and assisted them with their coats.

"Here is my card. Write down your questions, we can discuss them in a few days when we get together, or feel free to call me if you need answers right away."

They left the funeral home in silence, the parents arm in arm. Jennifer reached out and gently touched Victoria's elbow as they left. Victoria had said very little during the arrangements, she had been focused on her parents. Jennifer was stuck by the young woman's maturity and attentiveness to her mom.

"I'll talk to you soon, take care," she said.

The daughter looked at her, her eyes reflecting her exhaustion and grief. "Thanks."

Jennifer stood beside the front window out of sight, where she often stood when clients were leaving, and watched them drive out of the parking lot. The snow covered the sidewalk and lot. She had about half an hour to get ready before William, John's driver, arrived to pick her up.

"Maybe I should leave it," she said to no one in particular. As she started to close the door she changed her mind. If she left it, it would mean more shovelling later. Walking briskly to the garage, she put on her winter coat and mitts and started shoveling the front walk. The parking lot would be taken care of by a ploughing service. As she shoveled, she realized her first year as a funeral home owner was drawing to a close.

I've accomplished a great deal in a year.

The large sum of money found in a casket her first week in the funeral home, and her kidnapping, had challenged everything she held dear. But then, so much good had happened too. Smiling as she reflected on her year, Jennifer shoveled with renewed vigour, until the sidewalks were clear. Winter was her favourite season. Her cheeks were rosy from the cold and, feeling invigorated, she surveyed her work.

"Is this what I want to do for the rest of my life?" she asked herself out loud.

She walked to the garage and put the shovel away, took off her coat and mitts and went to the lounge to shut it down. Glancing at her phone, she realized time was not her friend, she needed to hustle. Casting a critical eye around the lounge, she picked up the cups and gathered them for washing.

"Yes." No one heard her or responded. She was alone. "Absolutely." Her mind went to the family she had just served.

Not too many people have the privilege of being able to help others through such a tragic time in their lives. I'm fortunate to be able to do what matters to me and hopefully to them.

2

John Wisener's driver drove up just as Jennifer finished in the lounge. Opening the front door, she waved at William, and raced up the stairs to get ready.

"I wouldn't trade places with anyone," she said out loud again as she bent down and scooped up her cat. Grimsby purred loudly in her arms as she scratched under his chin and gave him a quick squeeze.

"If purrs could bring peace on earth, you would be a big contributor, buddy," she said as she buried her face in his fur for a few seconds before she put him on the couch. At least she knew exactly what she was going to wear to dinner.

Pulling out the red suit she'd worn as Marcia's maid of honour, Jennifer slipped into it in a flash.

Her stomach fluttered with butterflies as she rushed to get ready. She hated to keep people waiting.

"I'm going to take my red purse and wear my red shoes whether you like it or not, Grimsby. Jennifer hurried to the kitchen to collect the cookies. "No snow boots for me. It's Christmas and I'm spending the evening with a friend. So there!" She laughed as he yawned again and slowly closed his eyes, shutting her out.

Turning on the TV so Grimsby would have a bit of familiar background noise, she double-checked her makeup and hair, grabbed her coat, and hurried downstairs to meet William.

Stepping into the cold night, the click of her red heels were muffled on the freshly shovelled walk. She greeted William with a smile as he opened the car door for her.

"Merry Christmas!"

"Merry Christmas to you too, Ms. Spencer."

She handed him a wrapped parcel with her homemade cookies, tucked her new red purse under her arm, and relaxed in the comfortable back seat. Grimsby was settled for the evening, now it was her turn to focus on dinner with John. All the rushing around had left her breathless. William had Christmas music playing and, as she sat back, Jennifer hummed along with the familiar carols as they drove to the hotel.

When they reached the restaurant, William handed the keys to the valet and walked Jennifer into the building. The host took her the back room of the cheerfully decorated restaurant where a bright faux-fire cast its flickering light. The familiar table was set for two. John stood at the fireplace waiting for her. As she entered, he crossed the room.

"Thanks, William," John said as he took her coat. She could see the falls through the familiar floor-to-ceiling window. The snow had stopped and the world below, pristine and white, sparkled in the lights. It looked magical, like a picture on a Christmas card.

"Hello," she said, feeling awkward and shy. "Merry Christmas."

John looked handsome in a white shirt and red tie, a red sweater, and black pants. He smiled down at her and the butterflies in her stomach took flight again.

"You too, Jennifer." She felt a little like Cinderella and hoped midnight wouldn't come too soon. He leaned in and kissed her on the cheek. She put the parcel of cookies beside her coat while he signaled for the waiter.

"I hope you don't mind, I ordered wine."

"Half glass please." She smiled wanly. "I'm on call."

She walked over to the window to admire the view better. The Festival of Lights twinkled up and down the parkway and, with the fresh snow, the view of falls took her breath away. Pulling out her phone, she snapped a photo. Absorbing the scenery, she did her best to internalize it, wanting the memory to stay with her. She turned to John.

"Let's get a picture together," she said spontaneously. "It isn't every day one has a view this magnificent."

John smiled and obliged, putting his arm around her as they turned their backs to the window. He helped steady the phone as she snapped the photo, resulting in a perfect shot with the falls featured in the background.

"That's a great shot." John pulled out his phone and asked Jennifer to send it to him. He stood looking at it, smiling, before he put his phone back in his pocket. "I hope you don't mind, I ordered a proper Christmas dinner," he said as he held her chair.

"Gosh, it's been a few years since I had a proper Christmas dinner. Sounds fabulous."

And it was. They enjoyed roast turkey, stuffing, cranberries, mashed potatoes and vegetables. They ate in silence for the most part, savouring the feast, comfortable in each other's company.

"I just couldn't bring myself to order Christmas pudding for dessert," John said as he put his fork down and leaned back. "I hate Christmas pudding."

Jennifer burst out laughing. "That makes two of us."

"Is cherry pie a viable option?"

"It most certainly is. One of my favourites."

"Shall we have dessert and coffee at the window?"

Once they were settled again, Jennifer broached the subject that had been forefront in her mind.

"How is Winter?"

John's smile lit up his face. "Winter is thriving—she sends her love. She's been taking some university courses, she is happy and doing well. The baby is due in about six weeks. We've had some long talks. I'm so grateful to have her in my life."

He put his cup down and looked at Jennifer seriously.

"If you hadn't found her, we wouldn't be celebrating Christmas together."

She looked at him, puzzled, as his gaze wandered to the window and he fell deep in thought. She sat quietly, waiting for him to speak.

Turning back to her, he looked at her intensely. "You saved my life." Jennifer's face reflected her shock at his statement. "The last time you contacted me, I thought it was about the kidnapping and apprehending Mr. Holden. I was only too happy to assist, of course. But what you didn't know is that my despair and grief over losing Aaron..." He paused to collect himself.

"Let me put it this way. I am a successful businessman. To an outsider, I have it all. But when my son died, the grief overwhelmed me. About the time you called me, I had made the decision to end my life. I just couldn't go on."

"John..." Jennifer started to reach for his hand, then stopped.

"I know. You would never have guessed, no one would. But when you told me about Winter and my grandchild, it gave me hope and a reason to live.

At a loss for words, she could only study his expression. Her heart nearly broke at hearing that he had carried such heartache alone and felt it was too much to bear.

His comment that she had saved his life made her uneasy. *Why would he say I save his life? I was just helping Winter find her family. I had no idea he was at risk for suicide. I can't take credit for something I didn't do.* She pulled herself back to the conversation. There would be time to ponder his remarks later.

"The day you found Winter, you could have walked away from the ambulance and not looked back. Winter tells me she doesn't remember much, her despair and grief had overwhelmed her, too. But you persisted. You came to visit her with Chaplain Salinas and the police officer who was protecting you, and you wouldn't give up until you found out what had happened to Aaron." He stopped speaking and looked at her.

"I don't know what to say," she blurted.

"You don't have to say anything. Winter and I are indebted to you."

"I'm indebted to you too, John. You were responsible for getting Travis arrested and giving the police the information to bring down his network."

"It was easy. I have a security team capable of that level of work. Your commitment to Winter and I saved both of us, and her baby."

He leaned over and poured himself another coffee.

"Winter will be taking over the philanthropic part of my business, eventually. She's bright and personable and talented." He smiled. "Once the baby is a year old or so, she'll start working full time with the charities the company supports. She sent a present for you."

He rose, walked over to his overcoat, pulled a card from inside pocket and handed it to Jennifer.

Wordlessly she opened it.

Dear Jennifer,

Merry Christmas. I am looking forward to getting together with you soon, perhaps at the opening of the new woman's shelter in January, down the street from Williams Funeral Home. It would be an honour if you would name it.

I can't wait to show you pictures of the baby when she is born. John is beside himself with delight. I think I will name her Olivia Erin Wisener. What do you think?

Love, Winter

Jennifer dropped the card in her lap and looked incredulously at John. He laughed at the stunned look on her face.

"Yes, it's a girl. And yes, there will be a new shelter in your city. It's much needed."

Deep inside, tears of joy bubbled, then spilled out. She knew exactly what the shelter would be called. *Donna's House* after the woman who tried to get away from her abusive husband. There had been no shelter space for her when she tried to leave him, and he'd murdered her. She and Marcia would never forget that coroner's call and how it had impacted the front-line workers.

Unable to speak, she rose and threw her arms around John. "Thank you," she whispered, lingering a little before pulling away to sit down.

They sat in silence for a few minutes, Jennifer's head full of the excitement of knowing there would soon be a new women's shelter in town.

"Jim tells me he's met his match in your twin," said John, changing the subject.

"And the reverse is true. Jim matches her intellect—he's taught her a few things as well. The two of them can yak for hours. I just tune them out. I'm surprised though. Anne hadn't shown any interest, until now, in having a boyfriend. Her job is labour intensive, she's always made it clear that is how she wants to spend her time, and she likes her space. They do make an interesting and entertaining pair."

"What about you Jennifer? Do you want a soulmate?"

John's question threw her. They were just starting to steer the conversation away from her, and he brought it back around again. She pondered her response carefully and looked him straight in the eye. "I think so. But I chose funeral service as a career, and I love it. Past attempts at relationships have failed because of the demands of my job."

"Your friend Marcia is making it work."

Where is this leading?

The words were out of her mouth before she had time to articulate carefully what had been in the back of her mind for weeks, in the quiet hours when thoughts of work didn't intrude.

"She is, and I am thrilled for her. They share similar professions and unexpected work hours. *I* own two funeral homes…" She hesitated before she blurted out the next sentence. "But, there is someone I'm fond of." The emotional tension around them increased as he waited for her answer.

"You."

There. I said it. Her heart raced. She studied his expression, posture, head tilt…

"You don't think I'm too old for you?" he responded calmly.

"No."

"Neither do I. Jim says you are an old soul and I'm inclined to agree with him."

As they looked at each other, Jennifer finally knew. He did care about her. Her heart leapt for a second, before reality returned.

"Oh, John. It'll never work. I have my career. You have your business. Neither of us would be able to give it up for the other."

"Can we try?"

"How? I am truly sorry, but I don't want to live in a bubble. I feel your level of wealth will steal my goals and dreams. I want to be part of my community and be free to do my job."

"I would never expect you to become someone you don't want to be."

She looked at him, surprised he was searching for a middle ground.

"I, too, love my work," he said. "I also look forward to coming here and seeing you. From the moment I met you, I felt a connection I haven't had in a long time. I told you earlier I didn't think I could go on without Aaron. I have been able to move forward, but a big part of my life would be incomplete without you in it."

"And mine without you." Her joy at his revelation quickly faded. There were no easy answers.

"I won't be travelling quite as much for a while," John continued. "There's been a spike in influenza the past few weeks. I can run my business virtually until the flu season passes." He sighed. "My staff told me yesterday we're on the cusp of a pandemic. I'm positioned to be of service, as are you. If it happens, things will never be quite the same."

"I am obligated to serve," she replied. "It's not good news."

He rose and sat down beside her, drawing her close to him. She closed her eyes for a few seconds and allowed herself to feel his comforting warmth. John's words frightened her. She'd read enough history to know the seriousness of the pandemic threat. They sat in silence, staring down at the lights and the falls, content to be with one another.

"Promise me something."

Jennifer looked up at his intense and gentle face. "What?"

"Remember, no man or woman is an island. You put others ahead of yourself, which is a good thing, but sometimes it's to your detriment. You can't repair the world." He chuckled. "That statement, of course, won't stop you from trying." He looked into her eyes, willing her to listen carefully. "I will always, always, be there for you. You must let me. Promise?"

She nodded and he drew her back to him. They watched the falls in silence. She hadn't felt such joy in a long time.

But as "midnight" drew near, Jennifer broke the spell.

"I must be going." She pulled herself away from him a bit and, perched on the edge of the loveseat. She reached out and touched his hand. "If there is a solution for us, we will find it."

John nodded. "Neither of us are quitters. I want to be with you as much as I can. For now, we can simply try to see each other more often. Are you OK with that?"

"More than OK. I feel the same way."

As he texted William, and then helped her into her coat, she handed him the cookies.

"It's not much. I baked them this afternoon."

He took them from her, a big smile on his face. "Homemade? Wonderful! Thank you. Oh—I almost forgot." He reached over and pulled a little parcel from his coat pocket.

"It a re-gift. I spoke at a conference in Austria last week. This was the honorarium they gave me. I thought of you right away. I hope you don't mind."

Surprised, she accepted the parcel and opened it slowly, gasping at the contents.

"Wow."

Inside, on blue velvet, lay a silver and crystal Swarovski pen and pencil set. The light danced through the crystals and she touched the pen gently.

"It's magnificent. What a beautiful gift."

He looked almost shy. "You really don't mind the re-gift?"

Shaking her head, no, she put it down. Slowly, they leaned into each other and their lips met. Her heart fluttered as she breathed in his aftershave and melted just a little bit more. *So, this is how a first kiss is supposed to feel.*

A tap at the door interrupted them. John pulled away, made a face and opened it.

"Perfect timing, William," he said as he winked at Jennifer. "See you soon."

"Soon."

On the way back to the funeral home Jennifer clutched the gift in her hand, her heart rejoicing and her head racing. *If I gave it all up for John tomorrow, would it work? Could I live with that level of wealth? I worked so hard to get where I am, but...*

Before she knew it, the car pulled up under the portico and William was helping her out.

"Thanks for the cookies. What a lovely gift."

"You are most welcome. My pleasure."

That night, her thoughts bounced in too many directions for her to sleep. *Maybe time will provide a solution. Right now, I can't leave my funeral home. This isn't just a job, it's my true calling. My funeral home isn't just a business, it has become a community I've built up with the help of friends. Is that how John feels about his business? I owe it to myself to be honest. Right now, there's more at stake than just the two of us.*

3

The week between Christmas and New Year's passed in a blur at both funeral homes. Jennifer and Marcia and Peter were constantly busy as more flu-related deaths occurred. The same held true for Williams Funeral Home, and the teams at both locations worked together to make the best use of their time.

The Patterson family had Mike's funeral New Year's Eve. It was a small gathering with a few friends attending. Jennifer noticed that once again Victoria was especially attentive to her parents, her father in particular. There were no young people Victoria's age and Jennifer wondered if there was more she could do to support the quiet and withdrawn young woman. *I'll call Chaplain Clive or Chaplain Regina to see if they have any suggestions. I won't intrude on the family's grief or time today.* With that promise to herself, Jennifer concentrated on helping the family honour Mike.

Marcia provided the training for the staff that week. Over two sessions, she reviewed standard infectious practices and handling of deceased persons. She gave a brief history of the pandemics in the past century and what it meant for front-line workers and bereavement care personnel. Each staff member was given a copy of the Board guidelines for what to do in the event of a pandemic or mass fatality. At the end, Marcia surprised them by administering a test. Even with a few trick questions, everyone passed above ninety percent, proving to Jennifer that Marcia was the perfect choice for training officer.

The day after training, Jennifer took Marcia to lunch. She needed to talk to her friend about the situation with John. It had been playing on her mind and her mixed emotions left her unsettled. Marcia would understand.

As soon as they had placed their orders, Jennifer launched into the discussion.

"How do you and Ryan juggle your jobs? I know you haven't been married long, but the fact you chose to marry and commit to each other means you'll do whatever it takes to make it work."

Marcia's response surprised her. Instead of answering she leaned forward and asked, "Is this about John?"

"How…?"

Marcia interrupted. "Ryan and Jim are close friends, remember? We know John loves you. Jim picked up on it a long time ago. Do you care for him?

"Enough to give up funeral service? No."

"Did he ask you give up funeral service?"

"No."

"You need to figure it out, Jen. Your career aside, you didn't answer my question. Do you love John?"

Forced to face her feelings, Jennifer nodded slowly.

"Then what is it? Is fear stopping you? Distrust? Values? Morals?"

Jennifer dropped her head and pondered her response. When she raised her it again to look at Marcia her eyes glistened with tears.

"Fear mostly."

"Love and fear don't mix Jen. What are you afraid of?"

Her voice barely above a whisper, she answered as truthfully as she could. "I don't want to be like my parents. My mom gave up everything. She gave up her soul for my father. What did she get out of it? Nothing. She became a co-dependent enabler. That's part of it—a big part. Then there's his wealth. I can't live that way, in a bubble. I'm afraid of losing who I am, what I value."

"Do you trust John?"

"What do you mean?"

"Do you trust him enough not to make you feel you need to be someone you're not? Let me rephrase that. Would being with him make you someone you didn't want to be? And what does that 'someone' look like?"

Jennifer didn't answer. She couldn't.

"Ryan and I confront our differences, we even celebrate them. I chose marriage because I want children."

"I don't want children," said Jennifer. "Are you saying maybe I don't need marriage?"

"Did I say that?" Marcia had a tiny smile on her face. "You need time to make a decision. For now, enjoy what you have. Waiting for a bit will let you both know the truth about your feelings and the relationship."

"He should find someone who's rich and elegant and happy in a wealthy environment."

"But he hasn't."

"Not yet.'"

"But he hasn't," Marcia reiterated. "If he wanted to, he could have just about any woman he courted, or any woman who chased him. I bet they do chase him, or at least they chase his money. He chose you for an altogether different reason. You could be soulmates."

Jennifer pondered her friend's words. "Maybe." She sighed, long and deep. For once, the Scarlett O'Hara voice in her head remained silent. She wanted an answer, now.

Throughout the evening she picked up her phone half a dozen times and put it down, afraid to call John. Finally, her courage gone, she sent him a text instead, asking to give her a call when he was available. She sat half-watching TV, willing the phone to ring, until midnight. When it didn't, she went to bed feeling more inadequate and lost than usual.

He did call the next night, and once again she was left with conflicting emotions. They had a pleasant chat, and he didn't pressure her in any way. She had to find a way to get everything into perspective. So, the first week of January she drove down to the Falls, where she lingered in the Welcome Centre. A brief walk in the bitter cold had driven her inside where she got a cup of tea and stared out the window at the rushing water.

There were a few families and couples, tourists who had braved the cold to enjoy the view. She watched a young couple deep in conversation, leaning into each other. Their laughter and a lingering kiss made her think of Anne and Marcia and finally, John. For a brief moment she felt a tiny rush of anxiety. Marcia's chat about John had left her with conflicting emotions and the sense that she needed to make a decision. When they were together Christmas night, she felt safe and loved, and she wanted to do the same for him. *It shouldn't be so hard to make a choice. You can't have it both ways.*

The memory of their first kiss brought a smile to her face but her phone interrupted her reverie, demanding her attention. Her smile quickly vanished when she saw it was from the Public Health Office.

Heart pounding with a sense of foreboding, she rose and moved closer to the window, clearing her mind of John. Staring down at the Falls she listened intently as the Public Health Officer's secretary invited her and her managers to a meeting the following morning to discuss pandemic preparedness. She confirmed the time and tapped off, shaking with the reality of what could not be avoided. *This is a first call that no funeral director wants to face.*

A little frightened, she sat down again and pondered the situation. Peter had gone back to college the day before, to finish his first year. It would not be long before he returned, the colleges would be forced to close. Jennifer had left Elaine and Marcia setting up a suite—she needed to talk to them. Jennifer called Brent right away.

"William's Funeral Home, how may I help you?"

"Hi Brent, it's me. How are you holding up?"

"Not too bad, it's been busy for both of us. What's up?"

"We have a meeting tomorrow morning at the regional Public Health Office to discuss the influenza situation."

The silence on the end of the line spoke volumes. She could feel Brent's concern as she heard him let out a long breath.

"OK. What time?" His voice was measured and calm.

"8:00 a.m."

"I'll pick you up. See you tomorrow."

Jennifer went straight to her car, stepping around the young couple who'd stopped to kiss again at the exit. The funeral home staff had known this moment was coming, the influenza outbreak dominated the news cycle.

As she parked the car in the funeral home lot and opened the door, an icy blast blew the car door from her hand. Stepping out, the gust knocked her sideways and she grabbed the door frame. The wind overwhelmed her, slamming her into the side of the car. Steadying herself, she hurried inside, and leaned up against the doorframe to catch her breath and calm her racing heart. She was apprehensive, with good reason. *This isn't going to go away. We've talked about it and now it's time to act.*

Seeking out Marcia and Elaine, Jennifer suggested they go to the lounge. Her intensity projected a silent response from both women as they followed her and sat down.

Jennifer didn't preference the discussion with pleasantries. She got right to the point.

"I have a meeting tomorrow at the regional Public Health office." Both women looked at her, their eyes wide. They were experienced enough to know what that meant, and the fear reflected in their faces. Marcia sank back in her chair, eyes closed, exhaling slowly. Jennifer looked from one to the other, taking in the moment, the realization of how much they meant to each other sinking in.

"If this flu has reached pandemic proportions, we'll be doing six to eight months work in the next six to eight weeks. Do you want to attend the meeting too, Marcia? If one of us is side-lined with the flu…" Jennifer didn't finish her sentence. They were fully aware that *side-lined* could be best case scenario.

Marcia nodded and rose abruptly. "I need to talk to Ryan," her voice choking as she left the room. Jennifer looked at Elaine, her concern reflected in her face.

"You don't have to do this. I'll understand. This is a high-risk situation, above and beyond your job."

Elaine held her gaze. "It's not like we didn't know this was coming. It's been all over the news. It's you I'm worried about, Jennifer. We've all had our shots, we've done what we need to do to prepare for an influx of deaths. I won't be going anywhere." She walked over and hugged Jennifer as each comforted the other.

The hug helped to settle and ground both of them. Jennifer struggled to keep her fear at losing one or more of her staff to the pandemic in check as

Elaine continued. "I've known you for years. Every summer you'd come down and every summer I watched you grow from a scared teen to a capable and strong young woman. Some things, though, are stronger than we could ever be. I'm afraid you'll wear yourself out and get sick." Elaine teared at the thought. "I've been watching the news and flu-watch maps. None of us are safe. I could go and hide in the woods and not come out for weeks and still get sick. I'm staying. In fact, I made a list of supplies just in case."

"Good. I've been keeping a mental list, too."

"Then let's compare notes." Elaine linked arms with Jennifer as they went to her office. "We'll get through this."

Marcia joined them a few minutes later, looking a little pale.

"Ryan has already been briefed. The police were notified by Public Health officials yesterday that a pandemic is to be officially declared. He didn't tell me last night because he didn't want me to worry, but it doesn't look good."

"You don't have to do this Marcia. I gave Elaine an out as well."

"There is no out," Marcia said soberly as she squared her shoulders. Her voice steadied as she regained her composure. "There is only in. We are professionals and we are mandated to serve. It's our duty. Yes, I'll go with you tomorrow, and I'll be there for the duration. Now, we need to go over a list of supplies."

"Elaine and I are working on it. Let's see what we all come up with."

Together they placed a large order for necessities like body pouches and gloves, body suits and masks. Elaine called the casket suppliers while Marcia and Jennifer completed the list with other suppliers.

When they were done, they stopped for tea.

"I'm not going to lie, I'm scared." Marcia absently twisted the ring on her finger. "Ryan says they are expecting a high death rate. Apparently, this strain of flu is not selective. It's hitting everyone: young, old, healthy, and debilitated."

"I'm scared, too," admitted Jennifer. "I'm scared one of us could get sick. Our flu shot may provide *some* protection if they have the strain right, but it's not a guarantee. I'm scared we won't be able to cope with the volume of deaths physically or emotionally." She leaned over and touched Marcia's arm, the look between them reaffirming a friendship neither wanted to lose.

"We're all frightened," Elaine said. "We're facing something that hasn't happened on this continent in nearly a century. If you look back at previous pandemics…." Her voice trailed off as she choked up.

"It has the potential to change all our lives permanently," added Marcia. "I am going to do my best to take it a day at a time. If I think about the long-term effects of food and gas shortages, infrastructure failures, hospital bed shortages, I'll want to run and hide. One. Day. At. A. Time." It sounded as if she was trying to reassure herself most of all.

The rest of the day passed quietly as they worked together, each lost in their own thoughts. The afternoon visitation was well-attended. That caused Jennifer to realize, that in the event of a serious outbreak, public gatherings would be discouraged. They'd have to adapt so families could proceed with funerals with limited or no visitation. But they'd know more as events unfolded.

Later, after they said goodnight to each other, Jennifer slowly climbed the stairs to her apartment. She sought out Grimsby, burying her face in his fur. Despite the comfort he gave, she broke down into full-blown sobs. They would all suffer—everyone would be touched by the pandemic. She lay in bed, unable to sleep, tossing and turning as she mentally prepared herself for the days ahead. As she ran through the effect the pandemic would have on all them, she realized with a start that she had not called the hospital Chaplains about Victoria. It had slipped her mind. *Maybe I'll call tomorrow.* As she rolled over, trying to get comfortable, her thoughts returned to the meeting just hours away.

It was a quiet trio who trouped into the regional public health office the next day. Several officials were in attendance, as well as funeral directors and cemetery and crematorium staff from across the entire region. They greeted one another solemnly, aware of the serious nature of what they faced.

The auditorium filled quickly. Jennifer spoke with Mr. Whitney and Ronnie, two of the cemetery managers from the region. They, too, acknowledged their fear of the uncertainty ahead. Everyone attending seemed ill at ease, with many shifting continuously in their chairs. The air crackled with tension. Conversations were reduced to whispers.

The public health officer, Dr. Bolton, started the meeting reviewing influenza outbreaks over the previous years. There had been many, he explained, all of which had been contained by preventative practices. He clicked on a Power Point presentation.

"Like all flu seasons, this one has the potential to get away from us, and it has shown signs of doing just that. It is an influenza A variant with a predilection for all age groups."

Using a laser pointer, he pin-pointed the stats on the screen. It moved from yellow to orange, then elevated quickly to red, the highest alert level, a pandemic. "At this moment there are already pockets of activity in North America surpassing the capacity of health care facilities." He nodded at his assistant, who passed out information booklets to everyone present.

"We have already met with the health care professionals, long-term care staff and the police. It's now time to speak with the bereavement care personnel. I'm sure you have noticed an uptake in deaths at your funeral homes and cemeteries. We are predicting a six to eight-week wave. This appears to be the beginning—we strongly suspect the worst is yet to come. Here is the information you will need for the weeks ahead."

He turned back to the Power Point presentation. Every detail relating to mass death handling that was covered by regulations, Act and law were outlined.

Jennifer made notes of the part of the respective Acts she needed to review, to pass on to her staff. She used the Swarovski pen John had given her.

As the crystals caught the light, she thought of him and her throat tightened. She wanted to escape, to find a safe place with John where nothing could hurt them. But, that couldn't and wouldn't happen. *It's not who we are.* Snapping back to the present, she concentrated on Dr. Bolton's words.

"With the surge of deaths, you will work with municipal and provincial authorities to streamline death pronouncement and certification. One or more of you may be appointed to liaise with the Ministry and/or municipal officials to facilitate documentation. The coroner or our office may determine your level of involvement." He paused to take a sip of water. The only sound in the auditorium was the shuffling of papers. The air was heavy with dread and fear.

"Autopsies will be limited to a select few deaths," continued Dr. Bolton. "The hospital morgues will be expanded if necessary to include refrigerated transport trucks. Several arenas in the region have been designated as temporary holding areas.

"We have enlisted the help of the military to set up a regional mortuary operational team. This is where the funeral service personnel come in. It will be a contained area in one of the arenas with an embalming section and three or four stations, capable of running twenty-four/seven. The arena will be used to document the deaths after a designated individual has pronounced death. Families may be directed there to claim the bodies of their loved ones.

"A local funeral director will be asked to serve as the Team Coordinator. The military staff will ensure security and provide extra vehicles for transportation. The Team Coordinator will work closely with them. If necessary, the coordinator will pull in funeral directors from areas of the country that have not been hit quite as hard.

"The college funeral service program second year students will be asked to serve too, which they can do under the direct supervision of licensed personnel. The coordinator will also be responsible for the training and supervision of transfer personnel. Funeral homes will be asked to use the arena facilities for embalming. There could be delayed interment because of the volume of deaths and frozen ground."

Dr. Bolton paused again to take a sip of water and allow the bereavement personnel in the room to absorb the information. Papers rustled and pens scratched in the silence as notes were made.

"Storage is limited. For that reason, you may have to encourage families to choose cremation over interment. Cemetery personnel, you may need to review temporary vault storage, burial equipment for cold weather interment, and crematorium staffing twenty-four/seven should it be necessary.

"Your professional organizations have provided you with the guidelines for mass fatality management. You are responsible for implementing those guidelines in your respective fields. Finally, it is your job to ensure your staff are cognizant of precautionary measures. No exceptions, no shortcuts. Repercussions of negligence at any level can result in more illness and fatalities." He clicked off the Power Point. "Questions?"

Marcia and Jennifer looked at each other. No one spoke or raised a hand—everything had been answered, well, everything except how to emotionally deal with the reality. It was official. This was happening and every worker in the room felt the weight of responsibility.

"On the handouts you were given, you will find the phone numbers of various Public Health officials, police officials and hospital personnel who will be managing the deceased. From all of you I need your cell, office and home phone numbers." He gestured toward one of the officials in the room. "Please leave them with my associate here before you go. Ms. Spencer, may I speak with you please."

Jennifer's heart leapt in her chest. What could he possibly want from her?

"Stay close," she whispered to Brent and Marcia as she rose to speak with Dr. Bolton.

One-on-one he was not as officious as he had been during the presentation, he appeared more relaxed and engaging. He did not shake her hand and she realized a gesture they took for granted would no longer be appropriate.

"Nice to meet you, Ms. Spencer. I understand you have post-graduation training which included infectious embalming practices?"

I'm not the only one, why did he single me out?

"I do, Dr. Bolton, as does my colleague Marcia."

"I would ask one of you to make the decision as to who will be the Team Coordinator. I will meet with that individual separately for a few minutes if you don't mind. Your funeral home is the closest to the arena selected as the morgue facility, which is why you have been asked to take on this role."

"Certainly, please give us a couple of minutes. I'll be right back."

She pulled Marcia and Brent aside and explained that Dr. Bolton was looking for a co-ordinator with post-grad training who was close to the arena. Brent admitted he had completed his certification several years ago, but never had to use it.

Jennifer looked at him directly. "I've only used it once myself."

"Me too," responded Marcia. "It was a few years ago."

"Are you interested in being Coordinator?" asked Jennifer as she turned to Brent. She knew his answer by his facial expression. He had a family to think of.

"No, I can't, Jennifer. I'm sorry."

"Don't be sorry. Your family will need you."

"I don't think I'll be seeing much of my family over the next few months," he said sadly. "You know I'll make sure Williams' staff is in compliance and I'll help whoever co-ordinates in any way possible."

"That leaves Marcia and I." She turned to her friend. "You are a newlywed and you and Ryan will barely see each other as it is."

To her surprise, Marcia teared. "If you can't, I will," she said, supportive of Jennifer as always.

"I *can*. I just hope I'm up to the task. Ryan will need you. You'll need each other."

"You sure?" Marcia's voice was barely above a whisper as she composed herself.

"I'm sure," Jennifer said, with a strength that didn't match her feelings. She didn't want the responsibility. Without a family to think of, and for that reason alone, she returned to Dr. Bolton and told him she would accept the task of Team Coordinator.

"We won't be too long," he said. "Your friends can wait?"

"I'm sure they will. Excuse me." She returned to a sober Marcia and Brent. "Can we do coffee after we are done here?"

"Sounds good," Brent said as he sat down and started looking through the handouts.

Marcia smiled at her and raised an eyebrow. "Behave yourself," she said in a low voice. "He's not wearing a wedding band."

Jennifer chucked. How like Marcia, to make her laugh during the tough times. While Dr. Bolton was a nice-looking man, she hadn't even given him a second thought. She'd been too busy to barely even think about John over the past few days.

As Dr. Bolton led the way to his office, he introduced her to a public health nurse, "This is Sarah, she's the infectious disease specialist for the region. She'll be your liaison officer with our team."

"Hi Sarah." As Jennifer accepted the business card, she noticed Sarah was an attractive, well-dressed, woman. She scribbled her cell number on the back of her business card and gave it to Sara.

"This afternoon, I'd like you to meet with the military officer who will be assisting with the set-up of the mortuary." Dr. Bolton focused on Jennifer and though he stood behind his desk, no one sat. "Sarah will introduce you. You'll be meeting at the arena at 2:00 p.m." He turned and pulled a manual off his bookcase.

"This is a detailed outline of procedures for health care personnel. I'm afraid it doesn't cover funeral service, only the management of the deceased, but it should be helpful you as you organize your transfer teams. We are hopeful the temporary facilities won't have to be used to capacity. It would be a good idea for all the funeral homes in the area to make use of the arena. In the event the ground is frozen and the cemeteries cannot proceed with burial, you may have to step up staffing of the room you work in—what do you call it?"

"Preparation room."

"Preparation room," he repeated. "You will also be responsible for coordinating transfer teams and working with the hospital morgues in the event of overflow. For their safety, the transfer teams must work in pairs at all times."

Jennifer nodded There was a lot to do and a much to remember. Her stomach was queasy.

Sarah spoke up, "My job is to work with the hospitals and long-term care facilities. Most nursing homes do not have a morgue. Transferring bodies from their facility to the arena quickly is a priority. I may not be able to get back to you right away. This is a large region with several hospitals and a significant number of nursing homes. The region is known for its growing population of retirees. I will do my best."

"This is uncharted territory for all of us," said Dr. Bolton. "We have prepared for years for such an event but plotting a course of action on paper is nothing compared to living it. There are variables such as staffing, weather, available resources all pulled together to form a realistic understanding of the situation. Any input you have, any advice relating to mortuary services, would be appreciated. You can make recommendations as we go forward and in your report when this wave ends."

Jennifer nodded as she took it all in. She turned to the Sarah. "When I meet with other funeral directors, or make decisions, should I have you present?"

"It won't be possible. Email me with the details of what took place each day, if you can. It will help us with future planning."

"It doesn't look like I'll have much time to work with families or staff." Jennifer wanted to wrap her arms around her body and rub her arms, but forced herself to remain calm, parroting Sarah's professional demeanour. "It's important the directors understand their roles and let that trickle down to the support staff."

"If you do send me an email, I'll have an alert linked to your name. I can scan it to determine urgency and triage accordingly," Sarah said.

"Understood." Jennifer had quickly warmed to the confident nurse's manner and professionalism and allowed it to help settle her frayed nerves.

"Anything else?" Dr. Bolton added.

Jennifer looked at him soberly. "Is there a projected death expectancy?"

Dr. Bolton and Sarah exchanged glances before he spoke, "We think it could be three percent, possibly upwards of five percent of those infected."

"I'll see you at the meeting later this afternoon," Sarah reminded. "Go and have a bite now. It's important for all of us to remember to hydrate and eat when we have the opportunity in the days ahead. It may seem like a small matter, but it's critical if you're a front-line worker."

"Thank you, Dr. Bolton, Sarah." Jennifer did not extend her hand, but gave a slight nod to each. "See you later."

As she shut the door behind her, Jennifer closed her eyes and paused in the hallway. The task ahead was Herculean. She just hoped she had the organizational skills to manage it.

Brent and Marcia stood chatting with Mr. Whitney when she returned to the meeting room.

"Looks like I'll be doing the Cemetery Coordination," he said as he shook his head sadly. "In the grand scheme of things, six to eight weeks isn't long, but as it looms ahead, it feels like an eternity."

"My feelings exactly," Jennifer responded soberly. "We have a lot of responsibility for a lot of people."

"Dead and alive," Brent added as Sarah interrupted their conversation to fetch Mr. Whitney for his meeting with Dr. Bolton.

As the three of them walked quietly to the car, Marcia spoke first, "Mr. Whitney was the only volunteer for the position of Cemetery Coordinator. The rest were married and not willing to take it on. Oh, Jen, I really hope you don't get overwhelmed— either of you."

Too late, and we haven't had to mobilize yet.

Just then, John's words came back to her: *No man is an island. We will work together and do our best.*

Over coffee, the three of them were careful to ensure nearby customers did not overhear their conversation.

"I don't even know where to start organizing and mobilizing," Jennifer said. "The shock of what lies ahead makes me numb, even though we knew it was coming. I can't concentrate."

"Nor can I," Brent said as he stared into his cup. "It's terrifying."

"Maybe we can help you come up with ideas as you start planning. Maybe, if God is listening, this will all be a false alarm and it won't happen." Marcia barely got the words out of her mouth before large tears splashed down her cheeks. Jennifer put her hand on her friend's arm.

"Ryan said we have to have a serious talk tonight. We have to draw up our wills. He said we have a rough road ahead, not just because of our jobs, but because of this influenza. It scares me."

"I'm scared too." Brent's brow creased in a frown. "Lori, my kids, our friends, our colleagues…" His voice trailed off.

"For now, we can continue to work out of the funeral homes. I guess it depends on how fast this accelerates and how many die as to when that will change. I'll know more when I meet with the military this afternoon. It must be pretty bad if they have to use the military." Jennifer shuddered as a violent chill shot up her spine.

"You OK?" Marcia asked, tears still rimming her eyes.

"Someone just walked over my grave. Maybe it's a reminder I need to do my will too. Let's make a pact, OK?"

"What sort of pact?"

"A 'no holds barred' pact. Whatever happens, no matter how hard it is, we *must* be honest with each other. There's no rulebook, no guidelines, for what lies ahead. I have no doubt we'll give this everything we have, but in the event it overwhelms one or all of us, we have to let each other know. Deal?"

"Deal," Brent said. "I'll make sure my staff makes the same deal."

Marcia nodded solemnly in agreement. They finished their coffee with minimal conversation, their hearts heavy as the people around them laughed and talked, oblivious or uncaring, of the reality ahead.

4

As Jennifer and Sarah entered the arena administration area, they were met by a tall, dark haired man in military fatigues.

"Hello Sarah." He did not extend his hand.

"Jennifer, this is Captain Zacharias Barry. Captain, Jennifer Spencer. She will be your liaison with the funeral service personnel."

Jennifer looked up into brown eyes that masked any impression he might have of their first introduction.

"Nice to meet you. Let's get started, shall we." He led them down a hallway towards the main arena as Sarah excused herself to speak with the Sergeant at the desk. *There's nothing warm and inviting about the arena, even from the outside. It's stark and grey and minimal inside too. The only colours are the sports team ads.*

Jennifer looked up and down the empty hallways as their footsteps echoed on the cold cement floor. As they walked, Captain Barry continued the conversation, "I serve as a logistics specialist and have been seconded for influenza detail, as have all military personnel. Here's how we're looking to set up. The back of the arena and outside area would be walled for maximum privacy when transferring deceased persons."

Pointing for emphasis, he added, "Out this door, there will be a separate mess tent joined to one of the exits. The transfer staff, the administration and registration staff, and the bereavement personnel will be fed twenty-four hours a day when needed.

"Your team's section, Ms. Spencer, starts here." He spread his arms wide. "You have self-contained men's and women's washrooms and showers. You have an anteroom to gown and glove and mask before entering a sealed preparation room."

He turned to face her, his gaze steady and piercing. "Your staff must understand if they leave this area for any reason they have to remove all protective clothing and place them in the biohazard boxes. Cell phones will be left at the front desk, which will be manned twenty-four hours a day. If you need your phones answered, the desk personnel will do it for you and pass on important messages via the intercom.

"The only non-funeral service personnel allowed in the prep area are the biohazard team and myself or my designate. The biohazard team is trained to disinfect quickly between cases, allowing your staff to go to the mess tent for five minutes or so to have a coffee before the next case. There will be a desk in the preparation room for you or your designate to supervise the prep and double-check the cases coming and going."

He walked her through the rest of the spacious area set aside for the funeral service teams. It connected to the arena. "One of the biohazard team members, a corporal, will be stationed here to monitor the flow of cases in and out. And here we have the room where families can come and wait for one of my staff, or a funeral director to take them to identify their loved one if needed. Clergy or a chaplain will staff the family room when they are available. Over here is a desk set aside for Red Cross volunteers who will assist with transporting families. There's extra space out back for refrigerated trucks. This is the only arena set up for the region at this point. Let's hope it stays the only one. Any questions?"

Jennifer was pleased that the Captain had been so thorough in his explanations. But there was one unanswered question looming. Her voice sounded small in the large open space. "The funeral homes can manage the increase in cases at this point. How soon do you think the arena may need to be utilized?"

"From what I have been told by the federal public health team, and our top brass, we might have two weeks."

Jennifer's sharp intake of breath did not go unnoticed.

"In a very real sense this is a battle, Ms. Spencer. The enemy is a pathogen and it won't discriminate. I am here to help you and your team. It's my job. I have your cell number, here's mine. Call me anytime, night or day. There are no stupid questions, no detail is too small. We're a team now.

"I'm new to this, too. All of us who have been deployed across the country are. Logistics is a far cry from managing a mortuary facility, so I'll have questions for you as well. If the military had an Embalming Corp, you'd be my Lieutenant. Understood?" He handed her his card.

Lieutenant? Her hand shook as she glanced at the rectangular paper and once more reality hit her. His embossed name jumped from the card on the front below the Canadian Armed Forces Insignia.

She had seen the insignia many times when she went to the base to watch military events her father had participated in.

Taking a deep breath, Jennifer tried to focus on the little steps. She entered Captain Barry's number into her phone, and slipped his card into her pocket. Barry's comments gave her pause. She had a great deal of work to do in the next few days.

"Thank you, Captain. I'll have the teams ready and will wait to hear from you about a set-up time."

Driving back to the funeral home, Jennifer did her best to focus as she tried to think what her first order of business should be. The enormity of the tasks ahead loomed and a sense of inadequacy threatened to overwhelm her again. *I'm a Funeral Director, not an Administrative Director or a Project Manager. I'm way out of my league.* With no way out, the path could only go forward. And no one wanted to move forward in light of what lay ahead. The military involvement was a *precaution*—in the event influenza overwhelmed the health care system.

Maybe it won't be as bad as the worst-case scenario we're preparing for. We all have to face this. We all have tasks and days ahead that will seem insurmountable. Start with one step.

She sought out Elaine and Marcia once she returned to the funeral home. There were two new calls, both elderly individuals.

"Marcia has already met with the first family, and has an appointment with the second family early this evening. She and Jeff are transferring now. She mentioned to me that from now on there has to be two individuals transferring." Elaine shook her head sadly. "The gentleman whose family she met with while you were out, died of a heart attack. Marcia insisted on following the new protocols, though, and Jeff went with her. It's going to be a strain on our personnel if you guys have to double-up on everything."

"It is," Jennifer responded. "But we can't deviate. He may have been in the early stages of influenza. Unlikely, but a risk nonetheless. I'm going to have a chat with Jeff when he gets back. I have a job for him. I'll text him, but if you see him, send him to my office." She looked at her administrator. "Do you think you could draw up an ad for the papers in the region? We need to start hiring transfer staff."

"Yes ma'am. Desta and I will get right on it." Elaine gave her a two-finger salute, trying to be light-hearted. But Jennifer could see right through the façade. She sat down across the desk from Elaine and told her about the meeting with the Public Health Officials, the Captain and her new role. Elaine listened intently.

"I barely know where to start." Jennifer heard the slight quiver in her voice and blinked back the threat of tears.

"Setting up your transfer team is a good beginning." Elaine folded her hands together on the desk. "Marcia mentioned you would be coordinating the bereavement care personnel. Desta and I can arrange the call schedules, do the personnel records and payroll. Will you be receiving government funding?"

"Good question. I didn't ask."

"Leave it with me, I'll check for you. What will your next step be?

"Notifying the funeral directors in the area. I'll have to use the provincial directory and contact them by email, following up by phone. I should arrange a meeting with them, maybe in our chapel, in the next few days."

"I can help with both, so can Desta. We can get the email list ready, compile phone numbers and help set up a call schedule and notify them of the meeting."

"I'll ask Marcia if she wants to give the area funeral directors a refresher course in precautionary measures and ensure they have access to personnel, like extra transfer staff. With the increase in call volume, I might train the transfer staff and let Marcia work with the directors. Or not." She shrugged. "I just don't know yet."

"You'll figure it out," Elaine said kindly. "You always do."

The phone interrupted them. It was another call; another family needing to be seen. Elaine passed the phone to Jennifer who took the details and agreed to meet with them at 5:00 p.m.

"Marcia's family is coming in a five o'clock too," Elaine said. "I can stay and get the files and preliminary work done."

"Thanks Elaine, appreciate it."

Jennifer headed to her office to start the list of funeral directors in the region. When the list was compiled she stood up and stretched. She'd forgotten to eat lunch, and remembering Sarah's words, ran upstairs to the apartment to make a sandwich.

Marcia had returned and gone directly to work in the prep room, not stopping to ask Jennifer if she wanted to help. Sensing her friend needed to work alone, and have time to think about the days ahead,

Jennifer sat with Grimsby for a few minutes, talking quietly with him about her pending workload. He purred gently as she stroked his fur. She talked herself through her next project.

Heading back down she sought out Marcia, who was finishing up. "Got time for tea? I have some questions for you."

"Sure. I have a family coming in at five."

"Me too. I'll get our tea ready."

Marcia joined her a few minutes later, sinking into the chair with a sigh. "Sorry, I didn't get the message to Jeff. You wanted to see him?"

"I'll text him, maybe he can help with my transfer later this evening. I was thinking of making him the Transportation Coordinator."

"Hmmm." Marcia cocked her head as she thought about Jennifer's statement.

"Not a good idea?" Marcia had trained Jeff and worked closely with him.

"No, it's a great idea, Jen. He's conscientious and hard-working. I think he would do a great job."

"You don't think he's too young for the responsibility?"

"How young is too young?" Marcia chuckled. He's four years older than I was when I entered funeral service. He'll make mistakes, we all do starting out. I still do once in a while. But he's the kind of guy who admits when he wrong and works to fix it. Jeff's a good choice."

Jennifer exhaled with relief. "Thanks. One of my projects is now taken care of. Next, there are sixty-two funeral directors in the region. We… sorry… *I* need to meet with them to coordinate the team in the event we have to move to the arena. Captain Barry thinks it could happen in as little as two weeks."

Marcia looked at her soberly. "That soon?"

"Yes, unfortunately. The directors should get a refresher course on precautionary measures and the handling of infectious remains. Once we move to the arena, the protocols will be strict. I've been wondering if you wanted to teach the directors or would you prefer to teach the transfer teams?"

Marcia didn't hesitate. "I'd like to take the funeral directors. I'll be working at the arena too."

"I think I may have to work there also. I might have to work a night shift though if the coordinating position keeps me busy. I'll do the transfer team training. Elaine is running an ad, we'll start with five hires this week. I have no idea at this point how many people we'll need."

"Are you going to tap into retired funeral directors too?"

Jennifer nodded. "I've given it some thought. Perhaps they could help look after the funeral homes when the directors are on shift at the arena or serve as embalming assistants at the arena. At this point I haven't compiled a list of retirees. I'll have to get to it in the next few days."

Jennifer drained the rest of her tea, stood and put her cup in the sink. "I'm going to start working on the email to the licensed personnel in the region. What day would you like to do their training?"

"Saturday? If some don't come, we might have to set up a second training session on Sunday. I don't mind coming in both days. It's your weekend on call which means I can concentrate on preparing them for what's ahead."

"Maybe we should include a tour of the arena."

"Good plan. I'll order cake and cookies and stock up on cream and milk. It could be a long training session."

"Poke your head in my office around 4:30 or so, I'll need a few minutes to decompress before I see my family."

"Will do." The two friends went separate directions, each intent on her tasks.

Jennifer texted Jeff to ask him to assist her with a transfer later in the evening. He replied in the affirmative. She'd take the opportunity to ask him about accepting the Transfer Coordinator's role. She rummaged through her pamphlets in her file cabinet and found the one about transporting mass casualties. Jeff could adapt and modify it as needed. Then, she photocopied some of the pages from the manual Dr. Bolton had given her. Seeing the pandemic protocols gave her pause.

It took her quite a while to tweak the email to the other licensed directors in the area. She was putting the finishing touches on it when Marcia poked her head in her office promptly at 4:30.

"Break time. You haven't moved."

"No," she responded as she stretched and yawned. "Time is just flying by right now. There's so much to do."

"Come on, old girl," Marcia said. "It'll be there when you get back."

They found Elaine sitting in the lounge waiting for them.

"Hi Jen. I have the files completed for your family. I got your list, as soon as the email is ready I can send it out. I have used your email to get the replies with a bcc to Desta and I."

"There are bigger funeral homes in the region, with more staff, but I doubt they are as efficient as you," Jennifer responded.

Elaine blushed at the compliment. "Thanks."

As they chatted quietly about potential tasks, another call came in.

"This just the beginning," Marcia said solemnly. "My client died of pneumonia."

There was no time for further discussion, the front door opened and Jennifer's family entered. She took them into the small suite and was getting them coffee when Marcia's family entered. Elaine led them to the front office and helped Jennifer serve her family.

"If you have time, would you check the email to the directors? I think I've covered all the bases," Jennifer said quietly.

Elaine nodded and went to the workstations. Marcia had claimed the corner desk, leaving one for Peter and one spare. Elaine used one of the stations when the front office was busy. The smaller suite would also have to serve as an arrangement office in the days ahead.

By 7:00 p.m. the families had left, and Marcia and Elaine were getting ready to leave, too. Jennifer texted Jeff to tell him she was ready to do the transfer. She planned on sitting down with him afterwards to discuss the position of Transportation Coordinator.

She checked the van supplies and stepped outside to take a deep breath of cold air. Jeff arrived in short order. She didn't recognize his vehicle.

"New truck, Jeff?"

"Naw, just test-driving it. I was at the dealer's when you texted. They let me have it for the night."

"Are you thinking of getting a truck?"

"Yeah, I've put aside some of my salary and I think I might settle on this one. It's got all the bells and whistles. It even has a make-up mirror with a light on the passenger side."

Jennifer stifled a smile. Jeff would appreciate the mirror as he enjoyed fussing with his hair. She remembered buying her first car. It had a fancy sound system and she'd sing at the top of her lungs as she drove.

She subtly watched every move Jeff made during the transfer from the nursing home. He followed his training to the letter. Satisfied, she asked him to stay for a chat when they were done. He looked a little startled but she quickly reassured him.

Sitting down in her office he sipped a coke while she told him about the position of Transportation Coordinator as he listened intently.

"You will be supervising people older than you, if you agree to do this. But don't let it throw you. You have the skills, and you have the right attitude. Marcia and I have your back should you run into difficulty. It also means you'll always be on first call, unless you delegate to a deputy or two from time to time, which I strongly recommend. It could be as little as two weeks before we have to move to the arena."

Jeff sat back in his chair and exhaled slowly. She could tell he was anxious, his freckles stood out when he was pale.

"Brent told us it might be bad. Who knew the flu could be so serious?"

"Do you like history?" Jennifer asked.

"Nope, not really. Why?"

"Just wondering. If you ever want to read about it, there were three pandemics in the twentieth century. The worst pandemic, 1918-19, killed up to fifty million people worldwide. Other figures make it higher. They don't really know how many died.

He let out a low whistle. "You're scaring me."

"I don't want to scare you, Jeff. It's the last thing I would want to do. However, this is serious and we can't let down our guard for a second."

He nodded solemnly.

"This position is yours if you want it. Marcia, Brent and I have every faith in you. We will start by hiring five people this week. If you're free, I want you to help screen them."

"Thanks, Ms. Spencer. I want to talk to mom about it tonight. Is that OK?"

"By all means, please do. Can you let me know in the morning?"

He downed the last of his coke and stood up. "I'll stop by on my way to work. Brent said he might need me tonight if we get more calls. We got three today."

"So did we. I hope you can get some sleep. It's critical we take care of ourselves in the days ahead, and that includes eating and sleeping properly. Remember what I told you about appointing a deputy to help with the responsibility and the workload."

He didn't answer, he just looked at her. It struck Jennifer once again just how young he looked, and wondered if she'd given him too much of a load to bear. He seemed so vulnerable.

5

Forty-three directors showed up for the meeting on Saturday. The other nineteen stated they would be available on Sunday. The Board and the professional organization had sent out a reminder notice the day before that a pending pandemic meant bereavement care personnel were mandated to work with public health officials and coordinators.

Jennifer had put in some long hours after her meeting with Jeff. After six more calls, she and her staff were starting to feel the strain. Elaine came in to cover while Marcia and Jennifer worked with the first group.

After coffee, tea and cookies, a solemn group of funeral directors met in the chapel.

"Thank you all for coming. Some of you know me. For those who don't, I'm Jennifer Spencer and I am the Team Coordinator. There is a sheet with your names being passed around, please confirm all of your contact details and provide alternate phone numbers. If you cannot make your scheduled shift, please let me know. My phone number is in the email you received. There is enough space beside your names to put your shift preferences during the period we will be working at the central prep area. You will see the facility later this morning. If you know any retired funeral service personnel who would be willing to come out of retirement, I would appreciate hearing about them. We need all the experienced people we can find."

A hand went up. Jennifer nodded at the gentleman.

"There are two small funeral homes in my area—neither director has a computer or cell phone."

"I saw that in the directory, thanks for bringing it to my attention. I have contacted them both by landline. I am hoping they will join us tomorrow." She smiled at him, he responded in kind. His acceptance of her role as Coordinator and his smile gave her confidence a boost.

"We also have a coordinator for transportation. His name is Jeff. Details were sent to you earlier today in a separate email." She paused for emphasis. "We cannot this stress enough, precautionary measures must be in place at all times. That means, from now on, two people per transfer. There will be a pool of transfer personnel. It will grow as the situation evolves. I will do my best to ensure each part of the region will have transfer personnel at their disposal. Any questions?"

No one moved or responded.

"I will be back later. Marcia will be reviewing protocols with you."

As Marcia took over, Jennifer went to the lounge where Jeff was waiting.

"Elaine said there's only two guys here. Ten people were supposed to be coming in." Jeff looked a little apprehensive and Jennifer did her best to put him at ease.

"It's early, I'm sure more will show up. Let's get started." She stepped back to let him take the lead. As Jeff led the way to the front office Jennifer smiled to herself. Jeff had clearly taken his role seriously, he'd spent extra time on his appearance. Every hair on his head was in place and his mom had ironed his clothes for him. She suspected that over time, they'd likely stop thinking about such minor details and simply concentrate on getting through each day.

She gotten up early this morning to read the news. The national media had reported an increase in confirmed influenza cases. Other articles addressed and outlined the precautions people needed to take.

The flu map also showed a jump in cases over the past week—the zones had expanded. The Niagara region was one of the hardest hit in the province, ranking in the top ten in Canada. Front-line personnel and hospital staff in the hardest hit areas were reporting a shortage of beds and CPAP and BIPAP machines. According to the reports, pneumonia was the number one cause of death.

She stopped at the office to pick up the first two resumes and a checklist she'd set-up late the night before. She quick-stepped to catch up with Jeff and handed him the first resume. She asked the young man to follow them to the small suite she'd set aside for interviews. He nervously took the seat she offered him.

Introducing herself and Jeff, she went quickly through the check list. Jeff listened intently as she interviewed the candidate. *It wasn't long ago I hired my first employee. At least it's getting easier.*

When she finished the checklist, she asked him if he had any questions. He shook his head no. Smiling, she stood.

"Thank you for coming in. We will be in touch by tomorrow."

As the young man left the suite, Jennifer sat back down and turned to Jeff.

"I forgot to mention. Normally, I would shake hands, but it's not good practice now. It's a hard habit to break." She gave him an apologetic smile. "So, what do you think about our first person?"

"He is available twenty-four/seven," Jeff volunteered.

"Anything else?"

Jeff shook his head.

"He has no work experience and he's in his early twenties. Does that bother you?"

Jeff looked puzzled. "No, should it?"

Jennifer laughed. "I guess I sound like an old school teacher and maybe I'm too picky. Does it not seem strange to you that he is in his twenties and has never worked?"

"Not really. Maybe he lives at home and didn't need to. I'm his age and I live at home."

"Would you hire him?"

"Would you?"

"I might. The lack of any work experience gives me pause. He didn't even admit to doing volunteer work."

"Should we put him down as a maybe?"

Jennifer checked off the 'maybe' right below 'hire' at the bottom of the form and handed it to Jeff.

"Would you like to do the next one?"

"You do it, I'll watch one more time."

As they worked through all ten interviewees, Jennifer watched as Jeff's confidence grew. Several candidates were young females, and a few of the men were older. Once they were finished, Jennifer and Jeff sat down over tea.

"Good work, Jeff."

He blushed.

"Thanks. We have seven definites, two maybes, including the first person. We have to narrow it down to five."

"I'll let you make the decision. You can let the other two know they will be hired later if the situation warrants it." He nodded. "Check with Brent about taking time to do the training and set it up for Monday if you can. We'll do it together. I'll outline the plan for you."

"We have seven calls right now," Jeff said. Jennifer could almost see the wheels going in his head as he tried to sort out his priorities.

"Seven calls are a lot for just the three of you," she responded thoughtfully. "You'll have to distance yourself sooner rather than later from transferring all the time, from the looks of it. You might want to pick the candidate you want to work with you at Williams after training. It'll free you up to work with the entire team. Ultimately though, Brent may have to hire more employees."

Jeff had been listening intently. "I'll do that. Let's make sure I got this right." He went down the checklist of things he had to do.

"One more thing. You'll need access to a computer. I need everything in writing. You can use one of the workstations here. Once a day I'll need a report from you. You will need to cc Desta and Elaine."

"I feel like a real boss."

"You are a real boss, Jeff." The corners of her lips rose as she gave him a wry smile. "Bosses don't have regular hours. You and I will be seeing a lot of each other over the next weeks."

"I'll call Brent and let him know what's up. If there's nothing urgent, I'll use the workstation and get started."

Jennifer had just sat down in her office when Marcia knocked on the door frame.

"We're ready to go to the arena now."

"I'll be right there."

Jennifer sent a text to Captain Barry, told Jeff she'd be back later, and shrugged on her coat. As she went outside, she noted the parking lot looked like a funeral service convention—almost all the cars were black Cadillacs or Lincolns.

Marcia climbed into the passenger side of the car.

"How did the training session go?" Jennifer asked as Marcia waited for the other drivers to get to their cars. Some weren't familiar with the area and she didn't want them to get lost.

"There was some skepticism. I wasn't expecting that."

"Really?" Jennifer couldn't hide the surprise in her voice.

"Yeah. A few of the younger directors seemed to take it lightly. One mentioned he thought it was overkill going through the protocols, another one suggested all the preparedness was a waste of time."

"What did you say to them?"

"I didn't have to say anything. A couple of the older guys told them to read the news once in while, things were going to get very serious, very fast. That wiped the smirk off their faces pretty quickly."

At the arena, Marcia waited at the door for the directors to park their cars, while Jennifer chatted quietly with Captain Barry. As the group lined up outside, the Captain introduced himself and re-introduced Jennifer. Together, the two of them led the quiet group of directors through the facility as he explained how it would be set up. At the end of the tour, Jennifer asked if there were any questions.

"What if we have bad weather? Do we have to drive across the region to do a shift?"

"Yes, if possible," Jennifer responded. Captain Barry nodded in agreement.

"Worst case scenario? Call Jennifer, she will get in touch with me, and we'll send a vehicle for you. I have yet to know if I'll have enough staff to have a full-time driver in place, but we'll work it out."

With no more questions asked, Jennifer thanked them for coming and announced she would be in touch with a schedule when warranted. As they trickled out to their cars, she turned to Captain Barry.

"Thank you, sir," she said lightly, pleased they had worked as a smooth team. "I'll see you tomorrow with the next group."

"I've been thinking," he said. "*You* might warrant a full-time driver, unless you want to manage on your own for now. I have the same option myself that I may utilize it if the situation arises."

"I'll let you know." She thought it odd he mentioned it. Why would she need a driver when she could get around by herself?

It was as if he read her mind.

"Gas shortages, vandalism, people get desperate if there's a food shortage or the banks are closed. Your funeral car is a Cadillac. Someone might try to rob you. At least with a military vehicle and driver, they'll give you a wide berth."

She looked at him soberly. "I hadn't thought of that. Thank you, I will keep it in mind."

He nodded his goodbye as she turned to walk to the car where Marcia stood waiting. On the way back to the funeral home, she told Marcia what Captain Barry had said about utilizing a driver for transportation.

"Ryan did the same thing, he offered to have a squad car take me to and from work if they had one free. I still have my vehicle that I could use to get around. It's not as conspicuous."

"Is Ryan going to be home for supper?"

"Yes. I have an idea. Let's go out for dinner, just the three of us."

"Sure!"

"I'll text him." They had barely started chatting again before her phone chirped with a response. "He says he can meet us. Where do you want to go?"

"What about the restaurant where you had your wedding lunch? We could go for a walk along the falls and enjoy the evening after dinner."

"Sounds like fun. Let's do it." Marcia sent a text to Ryan, who responded immediately. "He'll meet us in half an hour. I could use a glass of wine."

"Me too."

A few minutes later, Jennifer pulled into the restaurant and they were enjoying their wine when Ryan walked in. Jennifer noticed how tired he looked and commented on it when he sat down.

"I *am* tired. The Lieutenant is off with the flu, there are a few other officers sick, it's been busy. No homicides this week, fortunately. How did the group meeting with the directors go?"

"Marcia did a superb job as usual. Jeff will be taking over as Transportation Coordinator and we toured the arena again. I like Captain Barry. He's solid."

Ryan had been listening carefully. "It's hard to think about, but daily we can see it coming. More and more people are missing work across the region."

The three of them talked openly about their respective responsibilities, comparing notes and making suggestions. Ryan's input was beneficial, he had some sound ideas about managing the staffing at the arena.

After dinner they walked along the falls, enjoying the winter air and the lights. Ryan and Marcia strolled hand in hand. Jennifer dropped back a bit and watched them, a lump in her throat.

I don't know what I would do without either of them. They're so happy together. John thinks we could have that ... but I'm still not convinced. At least, not in the same way. She sighed, then quickened her steps to catch up, determined to stay positive. There was no point in borrowing trouble.

She called John when she got back to her apartment. The two of them talked about the pandemic until midnight—not exactly a romantic walk but practical. He told her that with the increase in cases, it might be a good idea to forego the official opening of the women's shelter.

"Did you come up with a name?" he asked.

"Donna's House."

"I'll tell Winter. She can pass it on to the staff. We can have the official opening after this wave of the pandemic passes."

Both of them were silent for a few seconds before saying goodnight. There was no guarantee either of them could make about the shelters' official opening or the future. A microorganism might just make that decision for them.

6

Two weeks after New Year's, the increase in flu-related deaths put a significant strain on both funeral homes and staffing became a problem. Jeff had stepped up into his new position, exceeding expectations, as he managed a team of fifteen. That afternoon, he approached Jennifer about hiring another *twenty* people.

"It might be a bit premature, but I'd rather get them trained and ready. Some of the director's in the southern part of the region are struggling to keep up, especially when they have to do their own transfers."

"Can you manage the interviews?"

"I can," he said. "When can you train the new group?"

"Go ahead and hire. I'll make myself available to you as needed."

"Thanks, Jennifer." He headed to his workstation to get started, whistling softly to himself. Stopping in his tracks, he whirled around. "By the way, I appointed a deputy today."

"Good for you, smart move. Who?"

"Elizabeth. Remember her? She was one of the first five. Do you think I should include her in the interviews?"

"The quiet one with short blond hair and glasses? She only spoke when asked questions, didn't volunteer much information about herself."

Jeff nodded. Jennifer couldn't help herself, she gave him a big grin. "What do you think?"

He laughed as he responded, remembering how she kept putting some of the responsibility back on him. "I think she would do OK. She doesn't say much, she just does her job."

"Just like you?" Jennifer teased. Jeff blushed at the praise.

"Go ahead. I concur." She rose and picked up her laptop bag, pushing paperwork into the side of it. "I'll be at the arena, I should be back in about an hour."

Jennifer's cell phone rang as she exited the funeral home and climbed into the car. It was Peter.

"Hi Peter! How are you? How's Angel?"

"I'm good. I'm home. The college is closed until further notice. Angel had her doctor's appointment today. The baby could come at any time."

"I am glad to hear Angel is well. The news about the college though, that can't be good."

"The flu is taking a toll. It's on the news. All the colleges and universities in the province were shut down today. The public and high schools are shutting down tomorrow."

Jennifer sat back in her car seat and took a few deep breaths. "I missed the news today. I missed it yesterday too. So, it's finally come to that."

"Can you use an extra pair of hands? The professors briefed our class. We'll be able to return once this is over. In the meantime, we're being given apprenticeship status early. I can work at the arena or in the prep room under supervision."

"Are you sure? You have a baby coming."

"Angel is in agreement. I'm available. I have a classmate who's interested in working in the region, can you take him on too?"

"Of course. We need all the trained personnel we can find. Does he live in the region?"

"No, he's from Manitoba. He should be able to find a place to stay... he just wants a room until school starts again. I told him I'd help him find a placement. His name is Jordan. He's quite the character, the class clown, and in the top ten percent of the class."

"Brent could use the help, he has ten funerals in the next two days. I'll let him know. Thank you, Peter."

"I'll wait to hear from Brent."

"I'm sure it'll be soon, less than an hour." She paused. "Influenza cases are starting to accelerate quickly."

"They told us at the school to prepare for a high number of cases and deaths. I'm glad to be able to help. Talk to you later."

On her drive to the arena, Jennifer mentally reviewed the details she wanted to go over with Captain Barry. Her thoughts were so intense it seemed she arrived in seconds, not minutes. It was a brief and productive meeting with the Captain. She was comfortable working with the reticent man, whose attention to detail rivaled her own. Together they finalized the set-up at the arena and arranged to start transferring bodies within twenty-four hours—not only a sobering thought, but frightening.

On the way back to the funeral home Jennifer stopped at the grocery store, having prepared a list of non-perishable food items. She put her provisions into her trunk, then went back in to stock up on bottled water. She decided to make a second trip to the store after dropping off her first load of supplies, putting away enough provisions for eight weeks. On her second run, she heard someone approach from behind.

"Jennifer?"

She turned to see Victoria Patterson, her client from Christmas who'd lost her brother. A wave of guilt swept over her. She had not called the Chaplain's for advice, nor had she called the girl to check in on her. It had completely slipped her mind.

"Victoria, how are you? How are your parents?"

"Mom took Matt's death hard, she isn't functioning well. Dad sits in his office at home, calling in to check on things at work. Mostly though, he just stares out the window." Jennifer made a quick appraisal of Victoria's appearance. She was a little pale and appeared to have lost weight.

"And you? How have you been managing?

"I moved in with mom and dad to help out after Matt died. I haven't been back to university since. My professors are sympathetic. It's my last semester and my thesis is nearly done. I just don't have the heart for it right now."

"What is your area of study?"

"Organic chemistry." Jennifer's eyebrows shot up and Victoria chuckled at her reaction. "Chemical kinetics. I get it from my dad. He wants me to take over the business someday."

"Whew."

"Dad says I started playing with numbers when I was two. For as long as I can remember, he'd take me to work with him on weekends. I loved the labs and the white coats. I knew right from grade school that's what I wanted to do."

"You were born for it. Once the flu season is over you should be able to return to university."

"Yeah, I guess. It may be a while before I complete my studies though. Dad and Mom need me right now. Dad's cancer is progressing…" Victoria stared into the distance at his mention. "I should get back. I left a cake half-made on the counter while I scooted out to pick up vanilla. I need to try to return some normalcy to our lives. Thanks again Jennifer, you've been a huge help to us." With her free arm, Victoria leaned in for a quick hug, precautionary measures clearly not on her mind, and with a tiny wave of her free hand, disappeared down the aisle.

Jennifer finished her shopping run thinking about the Patterson family. Being successful and wealthy hadn't set them apart. In fact, they'd had more than their share of problems in rapid succession. *I just hope Victoria is able to get*

through this flu without further grief. She is such an
amazing young woman with great potential.

As Jennifer pulled into the funeral home lot,
after her second trip to the store, she noticed a truck
parked at the back. A young man got out when she
parked by the garage door. As he approached her,
she did her best to hide her surprise. It was Drew!
The employee she and Marcia had fired months
before.

He'd been a newly licenced director working for
the previous owner of Williams Funeral Home,
Dimitri. But Drew's girlfriend, Stephanie, took
advantage of Dimitri's illness and within a short
timeframe, had wreaked considerable havoc, turning
the funeral home into a mess. Cleaning had been an
enigma to Drew and Stephanie, who'd served as the
receptionist.

Jennifer and Marcia, having been approached by
Dimitri's wife to take over the funeral home, fired
Stephanie and reported Drew to the Board. His
licence had been suspended for six months for
infractions under the Act. Drew had stormed out the
day Marcia took over the running of the funeral
home, following an irate and upset Stephanie out the
door. But Jennifer knew Drew was still ineligible to
renew his licence.

However, the arrogant attitude he'd displayed the day Marcia fired him appeared to be gone. He approached her quietly, head down, only looking up when he was close to her.

"Ms. Spencer, can we talk?"

For a few seconds she didn't quite know what to do. "Come inside, Drew." She held the door open for him. "I'll meet you in the lounge in a few minutes. Pour yourself a coffee."

"Thank you." Those two simple words were spoken with abject humility. Jennifer remembered how Stephanie had bullied and abused him. Jennifer's intuition and his demeanour told her he'd changed.

She found Marcia in the office at her workstation.

"Drew's here. He wants to talk."

Marcia's face reflected her shock. "Why?"

Jennifer shrugged, making an "I have no idea" face. "Do you have time to join me?"

Marcia jumped to her feet. "Absolutely."

If Drew was surprised to see Marcia, it didn't reflect in his facial expression. Marcia sat down across from him, Jennifer sat to his left.

"What did you want to see me about, Drew?"

"I want to apologize for my behaviour and my attitude last summer. I've been reading about influenza pandemics and with a few weeks to go before I can be reinstated as a licensed director, I came to offer my services in whatever capacity you need."

Marcia studied him intensely. "Why should we take you back?"

Jennifer glanced over at her friend. Marcia's skepticism was warranted.

"You probably shouldn't. I wouldn't be here except for the pandemic. Being a funeral director is what I know. I want to help." He paused and it felt as if the room held its breath. "Please. I'll do whatever is asked of me. I can't sit in my apartment day after day and know I could have done something, anything."

"Excuse me for just a minute." Jennifer rose and went to her office. Placing a call to Williams, she asked Desta if she might speak to Brent.

"I'll put you through."

"Hi Jennifer. What's up?" Brent sounded tired. Even with the extra transfer staff, they were stretched to capacity.

"Do you remember me telling you about Drew?"

"Drew… Yes. The director I replaced."

"His six months are nearly up. Can you use his services?"

Brent didn't hesitate. "I can. Is he looking to come back to work?"

"Yes. He's here now."

"Send him over. I can definitely put him to work here. Gordon and I are running out of steam."

"OK, I'll let him know. By the way, the arena will be operational tomorrow. I expect we won't need a full contingent of staff for another week or so. But, I'll be sending out the email to the funeral homes in the region shortly."

"He can work as a prep assistant here until we move to the arena. He can also take first call for transfers. We've been running night and day."

"Exactly."

"Thanks."

Returning to the lounge, she kept her voice light, "I spoke with Brent, the manager at Williams Funeral Home. If you're free, you can start immediately. There is one thing though. You'll have to take first call at Brent's discretion. Have you had your flu shot?"

"Yes."

"And you are OK with first call here and at Williams?"

"Yes." His voice sounded tight, as if he afraid he might say too much.

"When did you last review precautionary measures?"

"I took a refresher course with the Board last week. I passed all the requirements to have my license reinstated. They'll notify me officially in two weeks."

"Brent is expecting you."

Drew rose and looked from Jennifer to Marcia. "Thank you, both." He walked to the front of the funeral home and out the door.

"Well?"

Marcia exhaled slowly. "I think he learned from his mistakes. I didn't want to warm up to him again. He really let us down. However, time will tell. We need all the help we can get. I asked him about Stephanie while you were on the phone. Apparently, she left him the day after we fired the two of them."

"I'm sure it came as no surprise."

Marcia responded with a raised eyebrow and a nod.

"I'm just about to get an email ready to send out. The arena opens tomorrow. It's time." As Jennifer heard herself make the statement, she felt almost detached from it and startled herself with the realization.

Marcia dropped her head and closed her eyes for a few seconds before wordlessly walking back to her workstation. As Jennifer started the email, she felt a heaviness she'd never experienced before—as if all the joy had been sucked from the air around them. She heard the front door open. Elaine would greet whoever it was. She needed to keep working.

Jennifer had barely finished her first draft before Elaine tapped on her door.

"There's a gentleman here by the name of Roger Stone. He is a retired director and looking to be of service. I just made him a coffee." Elaine looked at her intensely. "Are you OK?"

Jennifer nodded and looked up at her office manager. "As OK as any of us can be. The arena opens tomorrow. I'm almost ready to send the email to the directors in the region. It can wait until I see Mr. Stone."

"There won't be any good news for a long time," Elaine responded. "I'm determined to focus on the positive things people are doing to help others now."

"Speaking of others, Drew came by looking for work. Marcia and I talked with him. He'll be working with Brent."

"Drew? Really? Has it been six months?"

"Not quite, but he offered to help. Normally he wouldn't be allowed to work, but these are not normal times. Brent needs him."

"I'll add him to the schedule and let Desta know." Without another word Elaine returned to the front.

Jennifer checked her appearance in the mirror on the back of the door in her office. She brushed a stray hair behind her ear and went to speak to the retired director.

He rose as she entered the lounge, and extended his hand. She shifted hers behind her back and clasped them together.

"Thank you for coming in, Mr. Stone. Sorry, precautionary measures dictate we no longer have contact, so I can't shake your hand. Please, have a seat."

His face reflected his surprise as he slowly sat down.

"Common courtesy, Ms. Spencer. You no longer respect that?"

His abrupt tone caught her off guard. He was a grey-haired, bearded, well-dressed gentleman who resembled a department store Santa Claus. She walked over to the counter and poured herself a coffee, slowly adding cream before she turned back to him.

"Coffee?"

He shook his head no and she continued.

"I understand you are retired and wish to be of service. What did you have in mind?"

I am not going to let him intimidate me.

"I ran my own funeral home for forty-five years. There isn't much I don't know about the business, unlike some of the young ones I've met."

Not the most endearing person. Don't let him get to you, Jen. He's here to help and he's served a lot of families in his lifetime.

"Would you prefer to work at the arena or in a funeral home?"

"Don't want to work twenty-four/seven, I'm too old for the arena. I'll work in a funeral home. I live a few blocks away and I can walk here."

"Did you know my uncle, Mr. Stone?"

"Bill was a good man. He wanted to modernize, like all the rest of them. I had no use for modernizing. The old methods have worked so well all those years."

She knew from his last statement her next question would be met with resistance.

"Do you use a computer?"

"No"

"Cell phone?"

He looked out at her from under his bushy eyebrows. "I thought I made it clear I would be here to work. No, I don't use that stuff. Don't need it, don't want it."

He's scared. He's out of touch with the times and he doesn't know what to make of it all.

"No problem. We would be happy to have you here. Let me introduce you to my colleague, then we can discuss your hours. I will be out of the office much of the time now as the situation escalates. Excuse me."

She set her coffee on the table and sought out Marcia at her workstation.

"You look like the cat that swallowed the canary." Marcia raised an eyebrow.

"I have a 'Marcia' job. There's a retired director here. He lives a few blocks away and wants to help out in the funeral home. I thought you should meet him. In other words, he's your problem now."

"And...?"

"He's a bit of curmudgeon. Doesn't use a computer or cell phone, which is fine, a lot of people don't, just means we'll have to accommodate. He doesn't drive."

Marcia leaned back in her chair and rubbed her eyes. "All right. I'm sure he'll still be able to teach us a thing or two. I'll make him feel welcome and comfortable." She rose, stretching and yawning, and straightened out her jacket.

"Is a quick introduction OK? I can't visit, I have to get back to work."

"Of course." Marcia followed Jennifer into the lounge.

"Mr. Stone, this is Marcia. She is in charge of training new personnel and will be working with you here from time to time."

"Nice to meet you, Mr. Stone. Can I pour you a coffee?" Jennifer watched him smile warmly at Marcia as she reached for a cup.

"Yes, please young lady."

"I will see you later, Mr. Stone," Jennifer said as she left for her office. Sitting down, she stared at her screen, struggling to find the words she needed. Finally, her fingers hit the keys.

Dear colleagues,

The time has come to utilize the arena. At this point, we will be operating the prep room at one-third capacity and recommend all funeral homes utilize the arena for clients who wish to delay interment or have requested church, chapel or home services.

Nursing homes and hospitals transfers will go to the arena. Weather may affect cemetery services. In that event, disinfection will be required. A schedule is attached. Every effort has been made to accommodate each person's shift preference.

Sincerely,
Jennifer Spencer, Team Coordinator

She re-read and then added contact information should directors need to change their scheduled time. Elaine and Desta would take care of schedule changes if Jennifer was too busy. After attaching the schedule and finalizing the email, she went to the front office to let Elaine know Mr. Stone would be joining the staff for the duration of the pandemic, working exclusively at Spencer's.

As she finished, an email came in from Sarah at the Public Health office notifying her that all area hospitals had reached capacity. Temporary morgues would be put place in the form of refrigerated transports during the night. The military would be providing security. Transfer teams would be moving bodies from the truck to the arena initially. It was expected that the increase in volume would mean the trucks would move the deceased to the arena several times a day.

Jennifer forwarded her email to the funeral homes and to Jeff, clicked off the email and sat for a minute to settle the rising fear for what lay ahead.

Restless, she pushed herself away from her computer. Entering the lounge to retrieve her forgotten coffee, she heard laughter. Marcia and Mr. Stone were clearly getting along nicely.

"Hi Jennifer. Roger has been regaling me with stories of his adventures over the years. We reviewed precautionary measures. He mentioned he has some equipment and instruments in his basement. Since some of our instruments and an embalming machine are going to the arena, he would be able to utilize our prep room here for overflow, if that is OK with you."

"It would helpful, thank you. Elaine is in the front office. She needs Mr. Stone's information for payroll. After that is done, do you have time to take Mr. Stone over to meet Brent and his staff? It might be nice if he could put faces to names."

"Sure!" responded Marcia. "You up for a run across town Roger?"

"Yep." His response showed an enthusiasm that did not reflect his earlier mood.

Smiling to herself at the turn of events with Mr. Stone, who clearly had succumbed to Marcia's charms, Jennifer went back to her office to call Jeff. He was finishing a transfer with one of his new hires and agreed to stop by after he'd finished up. Two more calls came in the next hour and Jennifer arranged to see the families back to back. She emailed Sarah at the Public Health Office with updates for the day.

Jeff arrived a few minutes later and dropped a notebook on his workstation before sinking into a chair in her office.

"It's getting busy. I have three teams out today and between us there have been fifteen transfers," he said. "We are utilizing most of the funeral home vehicles as each home tries to keep up with their own transfers. To be honest with you, I think we may have to move to the military vehicles soon. The hospital morgues are full to capacity. Captain Barry is ensuring the trucks have adequate shelving as we speak. I'll need teams to cover the hospital overflow soon."

"How are *you* holding up?"

He looked at her intensely and paused before answering. Jennifer noticed he had an air of confidence about him she'd not seen before. "This is gut-wrenching work. More than a few times some of the team have broken down in tears, me included. I've had more people quit than I've hired. My mom says it's important to let it out and talk about it. It's hard though. When we do a house call and show up in protective gear, it's a shock to most people."

"Its important work and a sympathetic and compassionate transfer team is the first contact many of the families have with funeral professionals. You proved yourself working for us, now you're setting an example working with your team. Marcia and Brent and I are proud of you. I just want to be sure you don't burn out from overwork or emotional overload."

Jeff blushed at the compliment, as he always did when praised, the redness masking his freckles. Jennifer could see why Elizabeth could be getting sweet on him. He was a cute guy with an endearing personality.

"Thanks. I'll be careful. Elizabeth and I have some more interviews tonight. We can do those at the arena. I'll have your report ready in a few minutes. Elaine said to leave the ad up, she thinks we're going to need to be hiring regularly now."

During their short conversation the phone had rung several times. Elaine poked her head around the office door and looked at the two of them.

"Two more calls," she said, placing the information on Jennifer's desk.

"Marcia should be back soon, I'll pass them on to her. I have a family coming in shortly, and another right after."

"Desta told me they've had seven calls today, plus numerous inquiries. She also mentioned a friend of hers, a nurse, says there's a shortage of beds and staff already. The emergency rooms are inundated. The news outlets are covering it and telling people who have minor problems to stay away from the hospitals. That's all there is on news stations now, it's all about the pandemic and preparedness. The banks are telling people not to panic, the supermarkets are overwhelmed."

"I'm glad I stocked up with supplies and food," Jennifer said.

"Me too," Elaine responded. She started to say something else but the front door interrupted them. Jennifer rose from her chair and stretched.

"That's probably my first family. I'll use the small suite. I'll give Marcia the new calls when she gets back.

"Jeff, just email me the transfers you have done, I'll take care of it."

"OK, Elaine." Jeff walked over to his workstation.

It was nearly ten o'clock in the evening before an exhausted Marcia and Jennifer finished with the four families and had returned the numerous telephone inquiries that came in. Marcia wriggled into her coat and pulled out her keys.

"Ryan isn't home yet, I hope he ate something. Apparently, the Lieutenant took a turn for the worse and was taken to hospital earlier this evening. Ryan texted me to tell me not to wait up for him." She yawned deeply. "Thank goodness Roger starts tomorrow. See ya, kiddo."

"Night." Jennifer pulled up the news on her computer. An ominous article suggested the protein in the virus had shown signs of change, which would render the current vaccine ineffective in a matter of months.

Other articles educated readers how and why antibiotics were useless against viruses, and the media quoted hospital personnel who begged people to stay away if they were in the early stages of flu. An information hotline number for influenza enquiries flashed at the top of her screen as she flipped through news source after news source.

She clicked her computer off in frustration, not wanting to hear how many cases had increased in the past few days, or how many more had died. She didn't want to think about Anne, or her staff succumbing, or John for that matter. But she didn't allow her thoughts to linger there.

As Jennifer started to shut down the funeral home, she heard the front door open. It was nearly 11:00 p.m. Thinking Marcia may have forgotten something, Jennifer walked down the hall.

Mr. Patterson and his daughter Victoria stood just inside the door. One look at their faces caused Jennifer's heart to skip a beat. People didn't come to a funeral home at such a late hour without calling first.

Without thinking, she blurted out, "What's wrong?"

"Mom…" Victoria almost collapsed as she spoke. Jennifer was at her side in a second. "Mom's gone."

Inexplicably, Jennifer's eyes welled up and tears spilled out, her exhaustion and stress forgotten. Mr.

Patterson stood numbly, unmoving, unresponsive at his daughter's words. He had changed dramatically since the death of his son, his face now gaunt and drawn, his clothes ill-fitting. Jennifer took his arm and Victoria's hand, walked them into the office and sat them down. She chose a chair beside them and cried with Victoria—her tears for the remaining two members of the Patterson family mingling with the girl's.

Victoria had been strong and supportive of her parents when her brother died. Jennifer felt a connection with the woman, who was only a few years younger than herself, and who had suffered two losses in quick succession.

Her professionalism was gone.

Time had no meaning for the two Patterson's, grief had robbed them of more than time. The air was heavy with sadness. Eventually Mr. Patterson broke the silence.

"When we buried Mike a few weeks ago, my wife lost herself. She didn't want to eat, she couldn't sleep, none of us could really." He looked at his daughter who nodded. "Three days ago, she got the flu. It was like she gave up." Having broken his silent stoicism, he choked on his sobs as he spoke. "She'd been running a high fever. When I went to check on her, she wouldn't wake up. I called an ambulance, they took her to hospital but she didn't get better. They want to do an autopsy. I said no. I can't do this again so soon."

"I can't do it again at all," whimpered Victoria.

Leaning forward, her elbows on her knees, Jennifer buried her face in her hands. The impact of the Patterson's situation and her workload crushed her. But some part of her knew this was only the beginning.

Composing herself as best she could, she spent the next hour with them, agreeing to have them meet a chaplain at the arena to view and identify Mrs. Patterson before they transported her to the crematorium along with the dozen or so bodies in the truck. She didn't mention the truck or dozen bodies to them, it was too cruel. They didn't need to know.

As they left, Victoria turned to hug Jennifer, holding her like she was afraid to let go, the bond between funeral director and client surpassing normal boundaries. She watched Mr. Patterson walk to his vehicle with his arm around his daughter, observing them drive away before she shut down the funeral home and dragged herself upstairs. It was well after midnight. A disgruntled and lonely Grimsby met her at the door.

Scooping him into her arms she headed straight to the fridge to get his food. "Tuna or whitefish?" she asked him, trying to bring some normalcy to her empty apartment. She put the tuna under his nose. He ignored it. "Whitefish it is then." Once Grimsby had eaten, and she'd cleaned his litter, Jennifer put on her pajamas, made some toast and tea, and curled up on the couch with her cat beside her.

"Grimsby, we have a major challenge ahead. You won't be seeing much of me. I'll make sure you have lots of dry food and water, I promise." He purred as she talked to him, stroking his fur. Tomorrow would be the first shift of many at the arena as the area directors started working there. She wanted to be there early to ensure the first shift went smoothly and the appointed shift supervisor was comfortable with procedures. When she felt herself finally getting sleepy, she put her cup and plate on the counter, brushed her teeth and climbed into bed.

When Jennifer rose the next morning, she watched heavy snow fall and collect on her windowpane. Jennifer put on a track suit, bundled up, and started shoveling the sidewalks around the building. She waved at the snowplough driver pulling in to clear the parking lot. He drove up beside her.

"Morning Jennifer, you're up early."

"Hi Matt. I like to get an early start to my day."

"Are you using your car today?"

"I do need it, yes."

"OK, I'll plow you out first so you can get going." He immediately set to work clearing a path to the street. She finished her shoveling, ran upstairs and changed. Not long after, she left for the arena.

The morning shift of funeral directors trickled in, four in all, over the next ten minutes. She hoped it would be a week or more before they'd have to schedule another two teams.

Taking a deep breath, Jennifer went into the arena. At the far end of the ice lay ten bodies. She looked around but there was no one was in sight. She walked around the outside of the rink and stopped at the spot where the dead rested. The body bags, in various shapes and sizes were white, like the ice, basically void of colour. She shivered. The arena was not a private resting place for the unfortunate victims.

As she turned to go back, a noise behind her made her jump slightly. Whirling around, she saw Elizabeth and Jeff enter with another body.

"How's it going guys?"

Elizabeth deferred to Jeff.

"The night crew pulled most of these people from the hospital morgue and the trucks, a couple from nursing homes. I'm afraid the morgue is filling up almost as fast as they can get them to the transports. Elizabeth and I have to get back to the funeral home and catch up on the paperwork."

Elizabeth nodded as she and Jeff exchanged glances. She couldn't help but note he looked at her warmly, and she responded in kind.

"There's coffee in the mess tent, it should be fresh," came a voice from behind the three of them. They turned to see Captain Barry.

"Hello Captain," the three of them said simultaneously. It made him chuckle and the warm sound of his laugh drove a bit of the cold away.

"In that case, Elizabeth and I will be there in a couple of minutes," Jeff said as Jennifer and the Captain made their way to the coffee pot. The rich smell of fresh baking greeted them.

"Just pulled the muffins out of the oven," said a cheerful young soldier behind the counter. "Blueberry." He placed the plate of warm muffins on the counter and Jennifer and Captain Barry helped themselves. They took a table near the door.

"I see you're set up and ready to go," the Captain said. "How many teams will be working today?"

"Just two. If necessary, depending on how many more bodies come in, I have another shift on standby. For now, we should be OK. The director in charge will make the decision later today."

Jennifer looked up as Drew, Peter, Brent and another director entered the tent. She smiled at them. "Good morning."

Good-natured chatter filled the room as everyone got a coffee or tea and muffin and took a seat.

As Jeff and Elizabeth entered, Jennifer noticed Elizabeth looking around at the noisy group. She seemed uncomfortable with the crowd and moved behind Jeff. For a brief second her face seemed to flash anger as she looked in the direction of Brent and Peter. Jennifer glanced over at the table where they sat with Drew, then looked back at Elizabeth. Elizabeth had turned her back and pulled out her phone. She checked it, and whispered something in Jeff's ear, who nodded as she left the room. He picked up a couple of muffins, placed them in a bag and left.

"We have to keep moving," he said. "Elizabeth just got a text from one of the team who called in sick. There are calls waiting. She just stepped out to ring for back up. See you later."

The team kept their coffee break/breakfast short and entered the prep area ten minutes later. As Jennifer walked with them, she stopped short of the door and asked Brent how things were going.

"Peter and Jordan are a godsend at the funeral home. My wife's boss called in this morning with the flu, he wants her to go in and try to keep the office going until he recovers. I may have to change things around since the kids are home. I can work evening shifts here, Gordon can handle things at Williams with Jordan."

Jennifer nodded. "Peter we know, Jordan's working out well too then?"

"He's sharp. He keeps us laughing. Peter was right, he is quite the character. I'm glad to have him on board." He drained the rest of his coffee in a few gulps. "See ya later."

After a brief chat with Captain Barry, Jennifer went to the family room and sat on one of the couches. She needed to speak to Elaine about a few administrative details. Elaine answered on the first ring.

"Hi Jen. Roger is with a walk-in family now. Apparently, they were told the body is at the arena, or being moved to the arena. How's it going there?"

"Teams are in place. They'll have a full day of it. They will make the decision who their team leader will be. I suspect, for the most part, the teams will be pretty self-sufficient."

"Are you coming back here?"

"Eventually. We have a major storm blowing in."

"I saw that. We don't usually get this much snow, it's been a few years since I've had to shovel this much." Elaine chuckled. "I don't mind, I could use the exercise to get rid of the little rolls on my stomach."

"They don't show. You always look great."

"Thanks for the compliment." Jennifer could hear a hint of a smile in her voice. "I'll call if I need you. See you later."

As Jennifer tapped off, she looked up to see a familiar figure at the door of the family room. She jumped to her feet and walked over.

"Chaplain Clive. Are you working here, too?"

"For now. I go where I'm needed. The hospital thinks the Chaplaincy should be working with the families of the deceased here, not at the hospital.

They want the space for the families of the living. Regina and I will be taking turns here."

Jennifer looked fondly at the old Scottish minister. "Have you been given the grand tour?"

"Not yet, lass. I just arrived and some young corporal directed me here."

"May I show you around?"

"I'd be delighted." He unwound his scarf and shrugged off his coat. "Nice room, not what I expected," he said. "During the war, my father served as a chaplain. He told me stories..." His voice trailed off before he dragged his thoughts back to the present. "Chaplains didn't have it easy, then."

"Chaplains never have it easy," Jennifer responded. "This is going to test all of us to the limit. Let's start with the funeral director's area, then the arena and the canteen. We can have tea. Are you expecting a family?"

"Not right away, but apparently we won't know in advance. They'll be sent here once the hospital has notified them of the death. They're given a number to call before they come."

"I suspect it rings through to the corporal and Captain Barry's staff. Have you met the Captain yet?"

"A Captain you say? Aye, well, he and I were the same rank. I was a Chaplain in the Royal Army, a CF4. The Jock's didn't call me Captain though, some called me Chaplain and the toffee noses called me Padre." He chuckled at the memory, lost in thought. "The others called me any name they could think of. I didn't mind. They were like family. Eventually I was promoted to CF3, which made me a Major for a few weeks. That was just before my wife died in childbirth." He exhaled deeply and stared off into the distance. "Such a long time ago. I left the military after I buried my Rose and our baby."

Jennifer was mesmerized by his story. "What did you do after you left the military?"

"Nothing. I stopped living for a while. I kind of lost my way, no heart for chaplaincy. It took a while to find myself again."

At a loss for words as she looked at the elderly Chaplain, Jennifer's chest tightened at his sorrow. To lose his wife and child would be incentive enough to walk away from the ministry and never look back.

"What brought you back?" she asked gently.

"The unit I had been assigned to was deployed to the Brunei revolt. It was just before Christmas and toward the end of the Empire. One of the patrols was wiped out. Some of the bodies were never found. Disease took others. The tropics were hell. I spent weeks with the families at home, not as a Padre, just as their friend. I was still a minister, just not officially. They didn't care, we needed each other and I grieved with them and supported them."

"How did you get to Canada?"

"One day I woke up and told myself it was time for a new start. No rhyme or reason to my choice to come to here. I'm Scottish. I like the cold weather. So here I am. Course, these old bones feel the cold more than they used to. I could tell yesterday there was a storm coming."

They continued to chat as she showed him the preparation ante room and the administration offices. Captain Barry was not in his office. When they came to the arena they both stopped talking as they looked at the ice surface and the bodies lining one end.

"That ice will be full soon enough," Chaplain Clive said, breaking the silence. He turned and left the arena quickly. Jennifer was hard-pressed to keep up with the old gentleman as he strode out into the hallway.

She led him to the canteen where they found Captain Barry seated with several military officials. He stood as they entered.

"Captain Barry, I would like you meet Chaplain Clive, a former Padre to the Forces, Royal Army. Chaplain Clive, this is Captain Barry, he is in charge of the morgues in the region for the duration of the pandemic."

Both men stood tall and nodded to each other. The mutual respect was evident. Captain Barry turned to the other officers he'd been speaking with and introduced Jennifer and the Chaplain to them. They were provincial coordinators, ensuring the regional facilities were functional.

"Nice meeting you. If you will excuse us, we'll get back to work," Jennifer said. She and Chaplain Clive got their tea and went back to the family room. She glanced over at the officers as she left, they were deep in conversation.

"I don't know if I'm up to this," said Jennifer to Chaplain Clive as they had their tea in the family room. "I'm scared."

"Ahh, lassie, rest assured we all feel that way. None of us are up to it. It is war against an enemy we cannot see. We are all scared, including those officers we just met. We're all fighting for our lives.

This flu could kill any one of us." He looked at her from under his bushy eyebrows. "In my case, I work to heal the souls of the one's left behind. It will become harder and harder as more die. You face the grief and pain of the families you serve. You also serve the dead. I'll warn you, though. There will come a point when all the bodies will come to mean little or nothing to you."

He stared off into the distance. The intensity of his gaze as he mentally visualized his thoughts was palpable. Jennifer did not want to speak, it felt as if the emotion around them would shatter the air if she did. A full minute passed before he spoke again.

"You will never be the same."

7

The rest of the day was a blur of activity as Jennifer went back and forth between the funeral homes and the arena. A second shift in the arena came in for six hours just after dinner. Drew and Gordon were working together. She left her cellphone at the desk, then suited and gloved and entered on the pretense of watching the workflow. Mostly, she wanted to observe Drew. He appeared to be working smoothly with Gordon, deferring to him.

The first shift had completed twelve cases. The ice surface of the arena was nearly clear, a temporary situation as the transfer teams went to the hospitals to clear the morgues, a routine that would take place in the evening after the pathologists and coroners had done their jobs. The transport trucks with the overflow from the hospital morgues would arrive in the middle of the night. She was grateful the military had been tasked with the mass transportation of bodies, it would have been impossible for Jeff to co-ordinate it all.

As Drew and Gordon finished their case, Drew mentioned to Gordon he was going to go outside for a smoke. The storm had not let up. The military staff had been busy trying to keep the parking lot clear.

"I'll just be a few minutes. If I'm not back in five, send help." He laughed as he said it. "You might have to dig me out of a snowbank the way the wind's howling."

"Gotcha," responded Gordon as he went into the ante room to remove his protective gear. "I'll be in the canteen having a coffee."

Jennifer checked the logs with the supervising director. Once she saw the situation was under control, she went to the anteroom, removed her gear and washed her hands. Picking up her coat and retrieving her cell phone, she went outside to her car, head down against the wind, moving quickly to get out of the blustery snow.

It was almost midnight and she'd put in a sixteen-hour day. Opening the car door, she tossed her briefcase on the seat. As she started to climb into the driver's seat, a shriek, loud and long, pierced the air. She turned back toward the arena in time to see two figures struggling in the storm. Jennifer walked quickly toward them as one of the individuals fell to the ground. She couldn't make out faces, as they were unidentifiable behind the hoods of their parkas in the swirling snow. It wasn't until she was about twenty feet away that she could clearly see someone hitting a person on the ground.

"Hey! Stop it!" she yelled. The person standing turned and ran as Jennifer approached.

"Are you OK?" she asked as she got closer. The person did not answer. A dark blotch spread into the snow beside the still form. She dropped to her knees to see what she could do. The person gasped, clearly air-hungry.

A tiny glow in the snow caught her eye—a lit cigarette.

"Drew? Drew!" She rolled him onto his back and tucked her arm under his neck, lifting his head slightly. She saw the life in his eyes start to fade.

"Sh… Sh… Sss…," he managed to gasp out. With a long slow expiration, he took his last breath. Jennifer watched, horrified, as the last spark of life left his eyes. The blood in the snow was all she saw as she eased him down and grabbed his wrist. No pulse.

"I'll get help." She knew instinctively he was beyond help as she struggled to her feet. But that didn't matter. Every fibre of her being screamed for action. The door to the arena weighed a ton as she struggled to pull it open. Jennifer stumbled into the warmth. The sergeant at the desk looked up as she rushed toward him, her boots thumping in the quiet lobby. His eyes flickered over her coat. Jennifer refused to look down.

"Call 911," she gasped before sinking into the nearest chair, shaking violently. Although she worked with death, she'd never been present when someone died. The sergeant dialed the number and handed her the phone, eyeing the dark stain on Jennifer's coat again. He hurried to the arena door. A blast of cold air hit.

"There's been an attack. We need an ambulance." The dispatcher took the location information and let her know the police and an ambulance had been summoned.

"Is he breathing?" asked the dispatcher.

She choked out a 'no' as the sergeant came back in and stood in front of her, listening to the call. She looked at him in anguish, willing him to say it was all right. He shook his head no.

"He's dead." She handed the phone to the sergeant who confirmed the information, disconnected, then redialed. She could hear him speaking with Captain Barry.

When the ambulance pulled up five minutes later, Jennifer went outside and stood by numbly as the paramedics worked to revive Drew. She barely noticed the ambulance take him away. Someone, probably the sergeant, took her back inside and handed her a cup of tea. She spilled most of it on her coat, unable to control her trembling.

"Jennifer, what happened? Where's Drew? I've been waiting for him, I heard sirens." Gordon came up beside her. She did her best to focus on him as a police officer entered the arena.

"What's happening?" he repeated.

"It's Drew. Someone killed him."

Gordon's eyes widened as he dropped into the chair beside her. "Who? Why?"

"I don't know. I don't know." She couldn't control her body, the shaking, her quivering voice. She was vaguely aware someone had sat down beside her.

"Jennifer, do you know who the victim is?"

She turned to the soft, gentle voice. It was Sue, one of the detectives who'd been assigned to her protection detail all those months ago. She looked closely at Sue's face, and saw her concern.

Deep racking sobs took over her body as she attempted to answer Sue's question. Sue listened quietly and Jennifer told her she'd held Drew as he died—felt his life slip away. Sue sat down in the other chair beside her as Gordon put his hand on her shoulder.

"Take your time," she heard Sue say. "You've had a nasty shock."

Jennifer struggled to regain her composure. "Drew Chandler. He worked for us."

"I need to know, where is the person who did this? Did you see more than one?

Jennifer shook her head. "He ran off." Sue waited quietly beside Jennifer until her sobs subsided. "Did you recognize him?"

"No."

Gordon sat frozen with shock beside her.

"I'm Detective Sergeant Zeigler," Sue said to Gordon. "Did you see what happened?"

He didn't look at Sue. "No. I was in the canteen. I can't believe it. He just went out for a smoke."

"Did anyone see you in the canteen?"

"Yes, there are two teams here, we sat together. When Drew didn't come back, I came out here to look for him." He sat back in the chair, his hands clenched between his knees and stared straight ahead.

"I'll be back." Sue rose and walked away.

Neither co-worker spoke to the other, they were too numb. Jennifer was becoming slightly more aware of activity around her, it just wasn't registering completely. The sergeant at the desk continued with his duties, directing police personnel and answering questions. Slowly Jennifer's shaking subsided. Closing her eyes, she shifted in her chair. A normally reticent Gordon reached over and took her hand. She did not pull away. Where was the military security detail when Drew was attacked?

Time passed unnoticed until Sue sit down beside her again.

"Gordon, Jennifer, you're free to go home. It's certainly not protocol, but under the circumstances, the rules can be bent a bit. We have a fair bit of work to do here still. I know you've been putting in long days, you both need to rest. Gordon, I got your information from the sergeant. I'll contact you in the morning. You too Jennifer. We have a constable ready to take you to your respective homes. Someone will pick you up in the morning. If I'm not here, I'll be at the station. Your cars will be safe in the lot."

Gordon released her hand and, taking her arm, helped Jennifer to her feet. Arms around each other for emotional and physical support, they followed the constable to the car. Again, they shared the silence as neither spoke.

The constable dropped Gordon off first.

"Take all the time off you need," said Jennifer, pulling her mind into the present. "Don't come back until you're ready." He didn't answer. As he started to close the car door, she leaned over. "Call me if you need to talk."

He nodded briefly before he disappeared into the swirling snow and his apartment. She leaned her head back on the seat and stared at the roof of the squad car. This had been one of the worst days of her life. Watching Drew have his life torn away, to see his blood in the snow made it hard for her to breathe.

She didn't say goodnight to the officer, just went straight upstairs and ran a hot bath. She fed Grimsby and crawled under her covers, still shivering occasionally from the shock. Sleep eluded her. The haze of morning broke before she dropped off.

Marcia's call woke her. Jennifer jolted awake and grabbed her phone. Marcia had been crying, she sounded stuffy and her voice was flat.

"Ryan told me this morning about Drew. I'll be there shortly."

"Come on up when you get here, I'll leave the apartment door unlocked." Marcia tapped off immediately and for a few seconds Jennifer's exhausted mind didn't register fully what had happened.

Drew was dead.

She flopped back down on her bed and curled up into a little ball. Grief swept over her. Her apartment was cold, she hadn't turned the heat up the night before. For five minutes she remained motionless. Uncurling slowly, she rose, looking at the bed with a longing to crawl back under the covers and not come out. Grimsby rose from his spot at the foot of the bed, stretched and yawned and lay back down.

Fifteen minutes later Jennifer was dressed and had the coffee on when Marcia let herself in. Her eyes were puffy and red. Both cried as they hugged each other tightly. Marcia let go finally and pulled back. Grimsby, hearing Marcia's voice, came out of the bedroom and rubbed up against her legs.

"I can't believe he's gone. How awful for you to have been there when it happened."

"I held him as he died." As soon as Jennifer said the words, her chest tightened with the thought of watching him, and her tears flowed again. Marcia poured them both a coffee and set it in on the counter. She pulled out a bar stool and sat down, staring into her cup.

"Marcia, I've worked with dead bodies for years. This is the first time I watched someone die."

"Ryan said he's seen good deaths and bad deaths. Poor Drew didn't have a chance to prepare. He was stabbed multiple times. It must have been awful for you."

Neither girl spoke as Jennifer let her tears run their course. Finally, she composed herself.

"Who could have wanted Drew dead? Why?"

"Ryan said Sue notified his parents about an hour ago. They'll be coming down even though she advised them not too. Some of the highways are closed with the storm. They insisted. He suggested we could meet them at the hospital. The autopsy should be done today."

"It's still snowing?" Jennifer had no interest in opening her blinds, she didn't want the outside world near her right now. It barely registered that Drew's parents were coming.

"It hasn't stopped. He said to tell you Sue will be in touch by mid-morning. There is something else, Jen." Marcia inhaled slowly before continuing.

"Ryan's boss, his precinct Lieutenant, died last night too. Ryan needs to talk with you later. His wife wants the service here. He suggested Williams Funeral Home where there's more room. Would it help if I met with Drew's parents, and you work with Ryan and the Lieutenant's wife? Ryan will be acting precinct Lieutenant for now."

"Is that what you want to do?" Jennifer answered, aware the tone of her voice had no inflection, reflecting her emotional state. She was exhausted mentally, physically and emotionally.

Marcia nodded affirmatively. "It's too much for one person. I was supposed to do a shift at the arena today. Do you think we could get someone else to cover? I'm willing to switch if they will."

Jennifer looked at her friend with gratitude. Having Marcia step up to meet Drew's parents meant a great deal to her. She couldn't face them.

"Let me ask Elaine when she comes in. Whatever would I do without you?"

"Run?" Marcia suggested, a tiny smile tugging at the corner of her lips. Her remark was reminiscent of the day of the Werther funeral when one mistake piled on another. Jennifer forced a smile too, in spite of their shared grief.

"It feels strange to smile when one hurts so much," she mused.

"We should probably get moving. Roger will be lucky to wade through all the snow to make it here for nine. He has a couple of families coming in. I suspect you have to get over to the arena."

"Eventually. I think I'll wait until Sue interviews us and I meet with Ryan. I told Gordon to take as much time off as he needs."

"Can it get any worse?" Marcia said sadly as she slid off the bar stool and then walked to the patio door. Jennifer didn't answer the rhetorical question. They both knew it would.

"Come, look out the window," Marcia said brightly in an attempt to lighten the mood. "This is not the Niagara Falls we know and love, it's buried in snow." She waved Jennifer over, pulling back the blinds as her friend approached.

A sea of white greeted them as they looked out. The heavy snowfall had resulted in a significant accumulation.

"Wow. How did you get here?"

"Ryan drove me. He'll pick me up tonight. No point digging my car out, it'll only get buried again."

"Gosh, mine is still at the arena. I won't find it until spring." They stood quietly at the window staring out at the bright white scene. Grimsby blinked in the light, jumped off the couch and stood at their feet.

"It's pretty though, isn't it? Remember when we were kids? It was magical," Marcia said wistfully.

A plaintive meow made them both looked down as Grimsby joined them. He could not see out; the snow had piled up on the ledge. Marcia reached down and scooped him into her arms. "Look Grimsby. Do you want to go out and play?" Marcia chuckled at the look on his face as he studied the snow. He was clearly not amused. He reached his paw out to touch the falling snowflakes, gently pawing the glass as they eluded him.

"Let me get him fed and clean his litter, so we can get this day started." A brief shared glance between the friends spoke volumes, reflecting the pain that lay ahead in their respective day, both thankful for the other's support.

Marcia spoke with Elaine about changing her shift at the arena and told her about the precinct Lieutenant's death, as Jennifer talked to Roger about the families he was seeing. Three more calls had come in, Marcia would be taking two of those. Roger still had refused to learn to use the computer.

Elaine was especially patient with him, telling Jennifer she didn't mind doing the input.

"He's never been exposed to it, why stress him out? We're lucky to have him," she had said to Jennifer, who argued that Roger should try to learn. Jennifer had acquiesced, a little miffed Roger had refused to move out of his comfort zone. Roger had remained polite with her, he was doing his job. There was still a bit of discomfort between them and Jennifer had not yet reached the point of being willing to bend.

She called the arena and checked with the funeral director who was co-ordinating for the day.

"It's busy. The transfer teams unloaded a truckload last night," he said. "The area directors responded to your email and are bringing in their cases. I think it's time to step it up and put two more teams on."

Jennifer closed her eyes as she heard those words.

"Thanks," she responded. "I hope to pop by later, I might see you then. In the meantime, I'll start scheduling." She immediately got to work, calling down the list until two full shifts were booked for the next few days. She would book a couple more days when she returned from the arena later.

Her stomach growled, reminding her she hadn't eaten since yesterday. She trudged up the stairs, tired and overwhelmed, and made some eggs and toast. As she ate, she read the news on her phone. Essential services such as public transit, fire, police and hospitals were reporting large numbers of staff illnesses. In another part of the region, a group of frantic people had stormed a pharmacy, demanding antiviral drugs and antibiotics. There were significant injuries. It was the first sign of violence in the region.

"I can't think about that," she whispered. "I have enough on my plate right now."

She finished her brunch and slid off the stool. Grimsby heard her rinsing the dishes and came over. She dried her hands, scooped him up and buried her face in his fur, listening to him purr. As she lifted her head and looked at the winter storm, she felt a fleeting sense of cocooned safety.

Her phone interrupted the moment.

The police station was calling to let her know an officer was on his way to pick her up. She kissed Grimsby on the head, put him down and gave him a treat.

"Love you," she said softly. Jennifer nabbed up her phone, then went downstairs to get her coat. As she descended the stairs she thought of John, wondering how he and Winter were managing. *I should call him.* Deep down, she missed him. He'd be able to tell her how to manage the workload.

The police car pulled up under the portico within a minute of the call. Even though it was sheltered, the bitter, cold wind snatched her breath away as she went outside. She glanced up and down the street. *This storm rivals the one last winter when Peter and I did the first coroner's call.*

"Thank you for picking me up," she said as she climbed into the back seat.

"Orders," was the clipped response.

She exhaled slowly. *First responders are stretched to the limits of their endurance. Don't take it personally.* She remained silent for the duration of the drive to the station.

The officer let her out of the back seat when they arrived.

"Thanks," she said over her shoulder as she went into the station. She wasn't going to let every little slight get to her. Maybe he had lost a family member, or was working a double shift. *I should stop letting other people's moods project onto me.*

Jennifer saw Sue speaking with the desk officer when she entered the lobby. She couldn't help but notice how tired Sue looked. Marcia had mentioned over coffee that morning that Sue had worked on Drew's case all night.

"Hi, Jennifer. Come on back." Sue unlocked the door and held it for her.

"You look all done in," Jennifer said as they walked back to the conference room.

"I'll be going home when we're done here. In fact, I can drop you at the arena or the funeral home on my way."

"That would be appreciated. Is the station short-staffed right now?"

Sue's face saddened and her voice dropped.

"We lost our Lieutenant to flu *and* two other officers. There are a dozen or so off sick. We're stretched to the limit. All the stations in the region are."

Jennifer declined coffee as Sue sat down and flipped through a file. The door opened behind her and Ryan entered. He merely nodded at her as he took a seat.

"Start at the beginning, tell me what you saw," Sue said as she picked up her pen.

Haltingly, Jennifer gave an account of the night before. A few times she closed her eyes to picture the scene, trying to visualize what she'd observed.

When she got to the part about kneeling beside Drew, leaning over and holding him as he died, her voice broke. No one rushed her statement as she struggled through it.

"I have a list of individuals authorized to be in the arena, they are all accounted for. What direction did the person who fought with Drew go? Left? Right?"

Jennifer closed her eyes to visualize the scene. "I was facing the building, so it was my left."

"By the time the ambulance cleared and the first officer on the scene checked the area, the snow and wind had obliterated the footprints," Sue said. "Can you give me an idea of how much you think the person might have weighed? How tall? I can appreciate it would only be an estimate, a parka tends to hide those details."

Sue finished her questions twenty minutes later. Ryan had been so quiet the whole time, Jennifer barely noticed him. Sue rose to leave.

"I'll be at my desk," she said to Ryan. "I can drop Jennifer off when you're done."

As the door closed behind Sue, Ryan leaned forward on his elbows and rubbed his face with both hands. Jennifer sat quietly waiting for him to speak.

"I want to discuss the Lieutenant's funeral with you. His wife wants a full service. I'm not sure it's going to be possible."

"If you wish, I can call Sarah at the Health Unit. She's my contact there. I can have an answer fairly quickly."

"Please." Ryan leaned back in his chair and closed his eyes.

Jennifer pulled out her phone and took it out of meeting mode. There were seven messages waiting. She ignored them and dialed Sarah's number. They had stayed in touch via email as Sarah had directed. This was the first time Jennifer had to call her.

"Sarah speaking."

"Hi, Sarah, it's Jennifer."

"Hi, Jennifer. What can I do for you?"

"I am with the acting Lieutenant for the police division near me. The Lieutenant succumbed to the flu. His wife wants a police funeral. What would you recommend as a health officer?"

"I'm sorry to hear about the Lieutenant, please pass on my condolences. To be honest, I would recommend delaying any visitation or services until this round of influenza has run its course. All public gatherings, including church services, are being discouraged. There will be a media announcement later today. All non-essential businesses are being asked to close today."

"I will pass it on." Sarah had Jennifer's reports, she knew the arena was moving into full shifts.

"Is there anything else?" Sarah asked.

"That will be all, thank you."

Jennifer disconnected and looked at Ryan, who slowly opened his eyes and leaned forward again.

"Officially, no."

He nodded. "I suspected as much. I saw the report stating all non-essential business are to close. His wife is not going to be happy."

"Theoretically, we have five to six more weeks of pandemic cases. The Lieutenant's funeral can be held once we have the all clear. It'll almost be spring, but it would be a logistic nightmare to have a major funeral with this snow. As a funeral director, I would discourage anyone from considering it. The cemeteries can't dig graves, parking lots are smaller with the snowbanks, its slippery…" Her voice trailed off.

"Not to mention departments from across the province will want to send a representative to the funeral. That isn't going to happen with the staff shortages right now. It's what I needed to hear. I'll leave it up to you to tell the Lieutenant's wife. If she gives you a hard time, call me. She's an old friend." He abruptly got to his feet and held the door open as Jennifer gathered her coat and tucked her phone in her pocket.

"I'm sorry about Drew," he said. "Marcia is devastated. She was hoping this would be a turnaround for him."

"Me too. Guess we'll never know." Her words sounded blunt and unfeeling as she walked down the hall. She was beginning to detach from her feelings about Drew's murder. There were just too many other details to think about. Sue, now acting Detective Sergeant, and her team would work on finding his killer.

As Sue dropped her off at the arena, they barely spoke. Jennifer asked her about Haney, her boyfriend. Sue looked and sounded happy as she told her they'd become engaged and had set a wedding date for April.

"Thanks, Sue. Congratulations again. Get some sleep."

Sue gave her a tired smile and a brief wave as she pulled away.

8

Jennifer signed in at the arena's main desk and went immediately to the family room. Chaplain Regina Salinas stood at the door with a family. Jennifer nodded an acknowledgment and mouthed the word "later". She started to walk to the arena but felt her anxiety rise with each step. Stopping, she took a few deep breaths. She had to face it, not just today, but every day from now on.

Nearly half the ice surface was covered with bodies. She looked at a family staring into an open body bag, a corporal standing respectfully nearby. A transfer team came through the back entrance wheeling a stretcher. She abruptly turned and went back the way she came.

As she stood outside the arena away from the cold surface where the bodies lay, Captain Barry walked toward her.

"There you are," he said quietly. "Let's have a sit-down, shall we?" He didn't wait for a response. He led her straight to the deserted canteen.

Over a muffin and coffee, he apologized for not being available the night before. Jennifer didn't respond as he continued.

"This is a secure facility. No one should be able to get in without authorization. The night patrol had been seconded to assist the police with the roving gangs. It left us short-staffed. From now on, even family members will be required to sign in." He shifted his weight a bit in the chair while still maintaining his straight posture. Jennifer waited while he gathered his thoughts.

"As of today, everyone will have an escort to and from the parking lot. I'm so sorry about the young man's death."

"Did someone break into the compound?" she asked. She didn't add *to kill Drew* but it flashed across her brain like a beacon, causing her stomach to clench.

He shook his head. "We don't think so. The police are working with us, of course, but we also have to do an independent investigation. How well do you know the funeral and transfer staff?"

"I know some of them, most of the group last night I know. Why?"

"It seems to have been someone authorized to be here, military or funeral personnel."

149

Jennifer nodded. It would only be a minor nuisance to sign in. *But if that policy had been in place yesterday, Drew might still be alive.*

As they finished their coffee, more people entered the canteen. Rising, the Captain asked her to accompany him to his office. Picking up their dishes and placing them on the counter, she followed him past the arena. An eerie silence confronted them. She closed her eyes, not wanting to see the ice surface again.

Not soon enough, she sat across from him in his office.

"I received the schedule you sent with the full contingent of staff in the preparation room. At our present rate of growth, we'll be at capacity in the next day or so. Is it possible to encourage families to consider cremation? I understand many would prefer burial, it's traditional in this region as opposed perhaps to a metropolitan area, but it might help allay the potential overload."

Jennifer turned her thoughts away from the ice surface and looked Captain Barry in the eye.

"I will check with the cemetery coordinator and get back to you shortly." She paused before continuing. "Under normal circumstances, the family should make the decision between burial and cremation. It's not a funeral director's job to push them in one direction, but rather support whatever decision they make."

"These are not normal circumstances."

She looked at the Captain, whose face was expressionless as he returned her gaze. It hit her, he wasn't just make a suggestion, he was giving an order. He had every right to do so. Her opinion, or the opinion of her colleagues, was moot. Breaking away from his steady gaze, she nodded. Her opinion, although justified, had to be set aside.

"A second arena will be opened as a morgue, strictly a holding facility. The bodies will be brought here for prep, if necessary. Otherwise, they stay there until cremation or burial. It will be staffed with military personnel. I will ensure you have a pass in the event you need to assist with registration. Our team will do the transfers to and from the two arenas."

"Understood." She didn't add anything, there was nothing to say. She hoped she wouldn't have to go to the second arena often.

"One more thing. I think it is time for you to accept a military driver."

She didn't argue or debate the issue, she merely nodded her agreement. Drew's death and the report of roaming gangs were enough to convince her. "I'll drive my car back and park it in the garage. From now on I'll call when I need to go out."

After reviewing a few details about certification protocols, they parted ways. Jennifer went to the family room to make some calls. Regina was still with a family, so she took a seat near the ice surface instead. She started with Mr. Whitney, the cemetery coordinator. He answered quickly.

"Hello, Ms. Spencer."

"Hello, Mr. Whitney. How are you and your team holding up?"

His tone changed as he let his guard down. "It's become a struggle. Staff have been off sick. The storms and snow have stretched our storage facilities to the limit." He paused. "I got word that a dear friend of mine died this morning. I just spoke with him a couple of days ago."

The arrogance she was accustomed to from Mr. Whitney had gone. He was clearly exhausted and grieving.

"I'm so sorry." She was at a loss what to say next.

"I know," he said sadly. "I bury people for a living. It is usually just a job. This is hitting me emotionally and personally. There are so many deaths." He took another long, deep breath. "What can I help you with?"

"Captain Barry asked me to check to see if all the crematoriums are working twenty-four/seven. We need to encourage more cremation. The arena is nearing capacity and a second arena is opening."

"Almost, but not quite yet. A couple of retorts are not running twenty-four hours. I will check with the operators, see if they have the staff to run them, and send you the figures. I'll try to have them off to you in about hour."

"Thank you. I don't know what to say except, take care of yourself."

"You too. These are challenging times." He disconnected the call.

Tragedy can really change a person.

She checked with an incoming transfer team to see how many calls they had pending, and with the day's coordinator in the prep area. Her next stop was Captain Barry's office. He wasn't there. The desk sergeant mentioned he'd gone outside a few minutes earlier.

Bundling up against the storm, Jennifer put her head down as she stepped outside and trudged to her car. It would be buried in the snow after sitting so long. The whiteness assailed her senses and she squinted. Little colour broke the intensity of the stark, bright landscape in front of her. Across the lot, someone in a parka brushed the snow off her car. As she approached her vehicle, the person took a long reach with the snow brush and, with force, swished the last pile off the roof. The snow hit her hard, knocking her back a bit, covering her from head to toe. The remnants showered over her like flour sifting through a colander. A cold blob of snow clung to her face.

"Ack!"

The person cleaning the car turned around. Startled, they looked at each other. It was Captain Barry.

"Oh, my goodness. I'm so sorry."

As she looked at him, looked down at her snow-covered coat and back up at his shocked expression, laughter bubbled to the surface. Reaching up, she brushed the blob of snow off her face and shook it off her hand, watching as it plopped to the ground. The Captain took a step forward and, with tiny swishes of the snow brush, tried to make it right. His clumsy attempts to brush her off only made her laugh more. He continued to stand in front of her as she howled with merriment.

"One more swoosh like that one and you would have buried me," she gasped, leaning up against her car for support. A deep chuckle emerged from the embarrassed Captain and, in seconds, he too was leaning against the car, helpless with laughter. As they attempted to compose themselves, he took one more dramatic sweep of the brush at her coat and their peals of laughter rang out again. Finally spent, Captain Barry was the first to speak.

"I needed that." Without another word he pushed himself off the car and walked back toward the arena. She pulled off her mitts and wiped the tears of laughter from her eyes, watching as he entered the building. Digging her keys out of her pocket she moved to tap the key fob and unlock the door. Inside, Jennifer noticed that enough snow had been cleared by the hapless Captain for her to see out all the windows. She stared out the windshield at the whiteness in front of her as the car warmed up.

"We both did," she said with a little smile as she put the car in drive and flicked on the wipers. She felt the need to be alone for a while and drove to the falls. Most of the parking lots were closed and unplowed. She pulled into the nearly deserted casino parking garage and walked down the hill.

It was obvious from the lack of usual hustle-and-bustle that locals avoided crowds and the tourists knew to stay away. Once she reached the bottom of the hill, she trudged through the snow to the railing. The roar of the water seemed louder than usual, the snow muting lesser sounds.

Jennifer stood watching the rushing water, trying to focus on the details of Drew's murder. Was he a target because he was alone outside? Is that what Captain Barry thinks and why he wants her to have a driver now? With no answers forthcoming she stood at the rail for a short while longer before the cold got the better of her.

Trudging back up the hill, a tiny smile again played at the corner of her mouth as she thought about the incident with Captain Barry. It was quickly replaced by a frown as her phone vibrated—the long list of forgotten messages calling her back to reality.

At the funeral home she backed the car into the garage at the back of the lot, checked to ensure she had everything she needed from the console and glove box, and locked the garage door. She wouldn't be driving that car for a while.

Entering the warmth of the funeral home, she heard voices. There had been several cars in the lot she didn't recognize, and as she walked down the hall she noted both Roger and Marcia were with families. Walking to the front office she checked in with Elaine.

"Six families so far today. I believe there is a gentleman in the lounge waiting to make arrangements." Elaine sounded tired, as if she had little energy to push the words out.

"Are you OK, Elaine?"

"Just tired and a bit achy. I shoveled the driveway when I got home last night. It's been a busy week."

"I'm back here for the rest of the day. Why don't you go home and rest?"

"I hate to leave you guys. There's a lot to get done."

"Go home and rest. It'll be here when you get back. You've been working non-stop for days." Jennifer's no-nonsense tone got through to her administrator.

Elaine nodded and picked up the phone. Jennifer listened as she asked her husband to come and pick her up.

"Sandy's on his way. Here are your messages." She handed Jennifer a little stack of pink slips as the phone rang. Jennifer got to the receiver before Elaine. She raised an eyebrow at her office manager and made a shooing motion with her hand. Elaine smiled slightly and, picking up her purse, left the office.

When Jennifer had finished the lengthy enquiry from a distraught family member about pricing and services, Elaine had gone. Jennifer decided to let the phone ring through to the answering service and pick it up once she'd caught up. The answering service was also short-staffed and stretched to their limit, as unavoidably they were missing calls. There was nothing that could be done about it, the families would just have to keep trying.

She went through the lounge to her office and put the messages slips on her desk. She pulled out an arrangement form and with the Swarovski pen John had given her in hand, she turned back to the lounge. An older gentleman sat alone, staring off into space, his coat folded across his lap. She approached him quietly and introduced herself.

"I'm Jennifer, one of the directors. What can I help you with?"

"My daughter Claire died this morning. I need to bury her." He seemed to wince in pain as he spoke the words.

Sitting in the chair beside him, she started to take the details. When the father got to his daughter's date of birth, Jennifer noted Claire was only a couple of years older than her.

"Where did your daughter work?"

"Tim Horton's, the one a few blocks from here."

A strangled "no" escaped her. The father looked at her, startled.

"I saw Claire all the time. She was on drive-through."

The father nodded. "She loved her customers." Doing her best to detach herself from the shock of the news, she tried to focus on Claire's father. She explained the burial situation and gently asked him if he would consider cremation. He nodded in understanding.

"Burial can wait till spring. We have a plot, we can put her urn there."

Jennifer heard the front door open and dimly registered Marcia's voice greeting someone. Feeling like she was rushing Claire's dad, even though she kept her voice calm and even, she completed the arrangements and handed him her card.

"Please don't hesitate to call me if you need me."

"Thank you, miss." He rose slowly and, after helping him with his coat, she walked him to the door. The icy blast hit her and she watched him disappear into the whiteness, more than just the cold air causing her to shiver. She'd seen Claire on drive-through only a few days before when she'd picked up a coffee.

Marcia came up beside her.

"Hi Jen. Where's Elaine?"

"I sent her home, she was exhausted. I put the phones on answering service, I'll pick up the line now and get the file done for Claire."

"Claire?"

"She worked the drive-through at Tim's. The gentleman who just left was her father."

Marcia shook her head and closed her eyes briefly. "There are so many young people dying. I have a family waiting, who just came in, and I have a shift at the arena tonight. Hopefully we can catch a few minutes together, later."

"Tell you what, I'll make an early dinner. I have some spaghetti sauce in the freezer. You and Roger have been busy, you need to eat. I'll feed you first, then Roger."

"Sounds fabulous. Thanks." Marcia turned and walked down the hall to the small suite where her family waited. In the background, Jennifer could hear the incessant ring of the phone. Ignoring it, she went to her office, picked up the message slips, and went upstairs to her apartment to start the spaghetti. Only when the meal was organized did she put her mind to the list of calls.

As she drained the spaghetti, a tap at the door interrupted her train of thought.

"It's open." As Marcia entered, Grimsby leapt off the back of the couch and ran to her.

"Goodness, Grimsby. You'd think we hadn't seen each other in days," she said as she bent down to rub his ears. He wound his way in and out of her legs, mewling plaintively.

"Sit," Jennifer said as she put the cheese and two glasses of ginger ale on the island. Marcia slid onto a bar stool and looked at her plate.

"You don't know how much I appreciate this. It's been so busy. Ryan and I haven't had a meal together in a couple of days." As it was, Jennifer and Marcia barely said a word to each other as they ate. Sitting back and draining her drink, Marcia gradually filled Jennifer in on the activity at the funeral home.

"Before I forget, from now on, call the arena and arrange for transportation," Jennifer said.

"All right. Did Jeff get hold of you?"

"Possibly," Jennifer replied. "I've barely scratched the surface of the messages and I haven't

161

looked carefully at my texts today. I'll make him a priority after we have dessert."

She slid off the island stool and pulled a small cheesecake from the fridge.

Marcia's face lit up. "Oh, just what we need. How did you get that?"

"I stocked up on groceries a few weeks ago and have a couple of treats set aside for times like this. Tea?"

"Yes, please." Marcia watched her friend prepare the tea and put the cheesecake out. "How are you holding up?"

Jennifer climbed back onto her stool and took a sip of her tea before replying. "Sometime I feel numb. I make arrangements, I talk to people, but it's almost as if I have to put my emotions on hold just to get through. Sometimes I just cry. Drew's death slammed me. Every death seems to have stolen a piece of me and I don't notice until I slow down."

"Me too," responded Marcia. "Peter said the same thing. When he's transferring or helping at the arena it all becomes a blur. There's no time to absorb or process all the pain until you stop. Peter also mentioned Brent has been unusually quiet. I hope he's OK."

"Remember our promise to each other. When it gets to be too much, no holds barred, we have to let each other know we've had enough."

Marcia nodded soberly. "I haven't forgotten. Ryan is my rock. We talk about each other's day every night without fail, even if we don't have time to eat together." She looked at Jen soberly. "Hospital bed shortages, food shortages, fuel shortages, medication shortages—it's all happening. Crime is up. Business are shutting down. No family has gone unscathed. It's worse than I thought it could ever be. I am so tired, I just want this to be over."

"Me too."

Marcia was quick to reassure her. "I'll keep pushing and I promise you, if it becomes too much, I'll let you know, OK?"

"OK. Likewise."

"Have you heard from John?"

"We've talked a few times. He's busy too, ensuring that hospitals have enough equipment and supplies, and keeping an eye on his business." At the mention of his name, Jennifer felt a pang of loneliness.

With a tiny sigh of satisfaction, Marcia finished her cheesecake and tea. "You go, I'll do the dishes. I know you have a lot of calls to catch up on. I'll be down in a few minutes."

"You sure?"

"Positive. Now shoo. Grimsby and I have got this. I'll bring Roger's plate down to him."

At the sound of his name, Grimsby let out a meow from his spot on the back of the couch. Both girls laughed as Jennifer picked up her phone and went down to her office to start the administrative part of her day. Time was getting away from her more and more.

She'd barely sat down and closed her office door when her cell rang.

"Hi, Peter. How are things?"

"Good, good. Angel's in labour." He could barely contain his excitement. "Her mom is with her. It looks like this baby is in a hurry. I can't do my shift tonight, I'm sorry. I'm just heading home now."

"Oh, Peter, how exciting. Give Angel a hug for us and let us know."

"I will! Bye." He disconnected as Jennifer sent up a quick prayer for Angel and the baby, then pulled up the roster to find his replacement. After a few calls, she realized there weren't a lot of options. Illness, family deaths and exhaustion were taking its toll. She looked at her email inbox and the pile of slips on her desk and sighed. If she worked as coordinator in the prep room at the arena, she should be able to catch up there. She found Marcia in the lounge with Roger, who was just starting to eat.

"Guess what!" Jennifer couldn't hide her excitement.

"What?" asked Marcia.

"Good news. Angel's in labour. Peter is home with her now."

A smile lit up Marcia's face. "That's great! Oh, I hope everything goes OK. I'm sure he'll let us know."

"I'll work the arena with you tonight, we can leave together. Roger, are you OK here by yourself? Elaine went home."

"Don't you worry about me, I'll be fine."

"Thanks, Roger. Make sure you take a cab home and get a receipt." Marcia and Jennifer exchanged glances as she returned to her office. She'd barely sat down when there was a tap at her door.

"It's open."

Jeff poked his head around the door frame. "You busy?"

"Not at all," she lied. "Come in."

Closing the door behind him he sat down and looked at her.

"What's up?"

"Elizabeth's getting a little testy lately. I'm thinking of replacing her. I spent the better part of the day hiring college and university students to do transfers. I lose staff as fast as I hire them."

"Because of Elizabeth?"

"Oh, no, sorry, that's not what I meant. It's because of the work. It's so hard on people emotionally and with all this snow, it's taking a physical toll on the teams too. There are just so many sad stories…" His voice trailed off. Jennifer waited quietly until he was ready to continue.

"I think Elizabeth's getting tired. She's slowing down, doesn't really know how to use a computer, although she said she did when we hired her. I don't know. It's making more work for me. I have a guy I hired early on who seems capable of stepping up. He said he'd do it." Jeff slumped forward. "Now I just have to tell her."

"You're thinking like a boss," said Jennifer gently. "Normally, I'd suggest you cut her some slack, but these are not normal times. She's probably burned out."

As he looked at her, she was struck by the maturity he now exuded. He'd come a long way in the past weeks.

"Are you able to train tomorrow?" asked Jeff.

"I'll make time. If I don't show up, you do it."

"I'd better get to it. Elizabeth is inputting, or should I say 'hunting and pecking' as we speak and I have some calls to make. Thanks, Jennifer." He closed her door quietly behind him as he left.

9

Several hours later Jennifer was gowned and supervising the prep room, stepping in where needed so the directors and assistants could take breaks. She'd left her phone at the desk as required, ignoring some of the messages, just answering important calls as the desk sergeant brought them to her attention. There were several, not the least of whom was Peter, beside himself with joy. He'd arrived just in time to deliver his daughter himself, with the help of Angel's mother. He babbled on about the delivery and the baby for ten minutes, barely catching his breath.

"I called for an ambulance but they said they couldn't send anyone. They did put a supervisor on who talked me through it. Man, what an experience. There's just nothing like it!"

"You won't need to take Angel and your daughter to the hospital to be checked out?"

"Yes. Sort of. Angel's fine, she was a trooper. We do have to take our daughter in to be weighed and checked tomorrow. She's so small and perfect. A nurse called to make sure Angel was OK. The nursery and maternity are on partial shutdown, they're only taking emergencies. It's too risky to bring healthy people in. Once our daughter's been checked, we bring her back home." He choked up as he said "our daughter." Peter had confided to her he was hoping it would be a girl.

"Congrats to all of you. I'll let everyone know."

"Thanks. I'll be back in a couple of days."

As soon as she disconnected, she told Marcia. The entire room celebrated with cheers. Some of the staff didn't know Peter, but any good news was welcome. With the mood in the room lighter, Jennifer stepped out to call John. Winter had delivered Olivia the day before, John had texted her. She had responded with 'congrats!' and said she would call when she was free. She realized she hadn't called and a wave of guilt swept her. Jennifer slipped into the family room and closed the door. John answered on the second ring.

"How are you?" he asked quietly.

"Holding it together." Another lie, but at least right now it felt like the truth. "How are you and Winter and Olivia?"

"I'm doing well. Winter and Olivia make life bearable. I adore Olivia. She is beautiful. Everyone OK with Peter and his new baby?"

Jennifer laughed. "Peter might have to be scraped off the ceiling, but yes, everyone is fine."

"That's good to hear. You told me you were holding up, but the workload must be getting the better of you."

She hesitated before answering, keeping her voice positive. "Yes. It's hard to watch people grieve. So many have died. There just isn't time to process it all."

"I hear you. Are you taking care of yourself?"

"Yes." She couldn't tell him the truth. He'd send William over with the car and a steaming bag of food... not necessary. She just had to convince her feet to walk to the canteen. "Are you?" She didn't tell him it was impossible to think about herself much. It was a moot point, the work had to get done.

"I'm doing my best. There's just more work than time. I wish we could get together," he said wistfully. "I'll try to free up some time and maybe get down for an afternoon and evening."

"Sounds good." Her voice sounded hollow. She knew he wouldn't come. "I have to get back to work. Give Winter and Olivia a hug for me."

She closed her eyes briefly as they disconnected. *Why didn't I tell John about Drew's death and how hard it was to deal with? Probably because life and work has changed since the pandemic flared. There's no time to get together or work on a relationship.*

Loud voices interrupted her train of thought. It sounded like arguing. She pushed herself to her feet and went toward the source of the noise on the ice surface. The voices echoed over the bodies on the ice. She could hear Elizabeth and Jeff, mostly Elizabeth. Jeff continued to work while she berated him.

Walking around the outside toward them, Jennifer saw Elizabeth reach up and tear the mask from his face.

"Pay attention!" she shrieked. "You can't replace me. I quit." When he didn't answer, she threw herself at him, shoving him. The force she used caused Jeff to stumble backward and he fell full-force onto a body on the ice. She watched as Elizabeth tore off her mask and body suit. As Jeff scrambled to his feet after the hard fall, she attacked him again. Bigger and stronger, he grabbed her arms as they wrestled.

For a brief second, Jennifer watched as if in slow motion Elizabeth slam her gloved hand into Jeff's face, mashing it as he struggled to get her off him. As Elizabeth raised her arm, her coat sleeve slid down, revealing a tattoo.

"Stop it!" Jennifer screamed. Footsteps raced up behind her. As Elizabeth turned, malevolence was written all over her face. It took Elizabeth a split second to appraise the situation and notice the other person running toward her through the arena.

"I hate you!" she shrieked at Jeff as she turned and ran out into the night.

A corporal ran past Jennifer following the direction Elizabeth went. A stunned Jeff stood unmoving on the ice surface.

Jennifer went to his side, linked her arm with his, and led him off the ice.

"Eye wash station. Hurry." She pulled him down the arena aisle and into the prep area. Her heart thumped in fear. Elizabeth had broken the barrier and contaminated him. Elizabeth's contaminated glove was a fomite, Jeff's face her target. His eyes, nose and mouth were vulnerable entrances for the influenza virus. She turned on the eye wash station and held Jeff's head as he rinsed over and over as he slowly realized the extent of what happened.

He trembled.

Jennifer heard several people talking outside the barrier door as he stood up.

"Ms. Spencer," someone called.

"Coming!"

"Marcia, can you give us a hand out here?" Jennifer asked urgently.

Marcia stood at the other entrance and took one look at Jeff's pale face. He was soaked and dripping. She turned to Jennifer.

"I got this." Leaving Jeff in Marcia capable hands, she went out to find the Sergeant and the waiting Corporal.

"Captain Barry is on his way. Is the young man OK?"

"I think so. He should be able to join us shortly. Did you get her?"

The corporal shook his head no. "She got away from me somehow. She can't have gone far. The gate's been alerted, there's no other way off the property."

A police officer entered the front of the arena and the Sergeant went to greet him.

"I have to decontaminate. I'll be in the family room," Jennifer said. She needed to sit down. She was a little woozy, her legs no longer wanting to support her.

"Marcia, I'll meet you and Jeff in the family room," she called through the door. "I have to shower first."

"Understood. Jeff and I will join you there. I'm free, my assistant is just finishing up."

Fifteen minutes later they assembled in the now crowded room. Captain Barry's first order of business was to ensure no one had been injured. He looked at Jennifer first, then Jeff. They both nodded affirmatively.

"Start from the top please, Jeff," he said. The police officer opened his notepad and started taking notes.

"Elizabeth and I had a disagreement. She hasn't been pulling her weight lately and tonight I told her she was finished. She attacked me, knocked me down, and when I got up she rubbed my face with her contaminated glove." Jennifer could barely watch him as he spoke. She was afraid for him. When Jeff had answered all Captain Barry's questions, he turned to her.

"Ms. Spencer?"

"I was in the family room catching up on calls when I heard yelling coming from the arena. When I entered, I saw Elizabeth and Jeff at the far end of the ice." When she got to the part about the tattoo, Captain Barry stopped her.

"Can you describe it in detail?"

"It might have been a skull or a dark, round flower. I couldn't say for sure."

"Any colours?"

She closed her eyes to get a mental picture. "It was black or dark blue."

He turned to Marcia. "Marcia?"

"I did hear a shriek. I was finishing up and on my way to the ante room to decontaminate. I didn't see what happened."

Jeff had been listening intently. "Elizabeth wanted me to move in with her. She said she loved me. I told her no. And when she sulked and slacked off for the past few days, I told her she was finished." He looked at Captain Barry, his face stricken. "That's why she attacked me. I didn't know about the tattoo, she kept it covered."

Turning to Marcia and Jennifer he blurted out his next statement. "I didn't want a relationship with her. She obviously didn't clue in. I'm gay. I didn't tell you guys because I wanted this job. I liked my job."

Jennifer shivered as he used the past tense for *like*. If Jeff got influenza it would be assault, Elizabeth would have deliberately infected him.

"Jeff, it has nothing to do with your lifestyle. You're an exemplary employee. Your job is safe, your personal life is your own."

"Phil, one of my best friends, is gay. He's an assistant manager at a big funeral home in Toronto," added Marcia.

"This is a small town compared to Toronto," Jeff said. "I wasn't ready to tell people. My dad is ashamed of me." He looked miserable and sad. Marcia reached out and touched his arm.

"It's nothing to be ashamed of, not at all. We will not betray your confidence, Jeff. I'm glad you told us."

As the police officer entered the room again Marcia pulled her hand away and sat back. She and Jeff exchanged knowing glances and he visibly relaxed.

"Detective Sergeant Sue Zeigler is on her way," the officer said. "I have to go, there are several robbery reports and store damages to investigate. She asked you to wait for her."

"No problem," Captain Barry replied. "Stay safe."

"I could use some coffee, anyone care to join me?" Jennifer said as lightly as she could as the officer left. She did her best to hide her own trembling. Elizabeth, who'd seemed so quiet and gentle, was a vicious, vindictive young woman who'd stop at nothing to get her way.

Sue found the group of them in the canteen fifteen minutes later, and once again they went through the story. Finally, Sue told them she had all the information she needed as Captain Barry excused himself. He returned a few minutes later.

"No sign of her. There were footprints leading to the fence where the snow is piled high from plowing. Elizabeth must have climbed the snowbank and hopped over the fence. I have someone levelling the snowbanks at the fence line as we speak." He glanced at his watch.

"It's nearly midnight, I saw the night shift go into the preparation area. I'll have your driver at the front door in ten minutes."

"Thanks, Captain. I'll go and make sure the shift is fully staffed. I'll meet you at the front, Marcia."

"I'll do the same for my crew and pass off the vehicle. One of the guys can drop me off at home," Jeff said.

"You sure?" Marcia asked, her face showing her concern. "You had a rough night."

"I'm OK now," he responded. "I'll head straight home once I'm sure I have everyone on shift, and I'll get a new assistant in place by tomorrow." He smiled at her. "Thanks."

As they went their separate ways, Jennifer felt her phone vibrate again. She sighed and pulled it from her pocket. Anne was trying to reach her by text and voice mail. Anne's voicemail was short and to the point. "Call me, it's urgent."

A tiny knot of fear gripped her and she hesitated before shoving the phone back in her pocket. She needed to take care of business first. She could get back to Anne once Jennifer was in her apartment.

The shift supervisor assured her they had everything under control. With nothing else pressing, she met Marcia at the front. Captain Barry walked them to the vehicle and opened the door for them.

"Get some sleep, ladies."

"You too, Captain," Marcia responded. As the vehicle cleared the gate, she put her head back on the seat and closed her eyes.

"I can't believe Elizabeth did that to Jeff. I just can't get my head around it. She fooled us all."

"Me, either." Jennifer's mind reeled with details, foremost Anne's call. She had put Elizabeth out of her mind.

The driver dropped Jennifer off first. She said a quick goodnight and unlocked the door. As she stepped inside, she pulled her phone out and hit Anne's number. Anne answered immediately.

"What's up?" Jennifer said quietly.

Anne was slow to respond and Jennifer's heart thumped in fear. Jim was forefront in her thoughts.

"Dad's dead. Mom called me earlier this evening. It was the flu."

For a brief second a thought flashed through her mind. *Is that all?* Her parents were not part of her life. Guilt swept over her as fast as the thought had hit.

"How's mom?"

"She was close to hysteria. Wanted me to tell her what to do."

"What *did* you tell her?"

"I told her I'd let you know. I also told her to work with her lawyer, they'd help her. She wanted to know if we could go up and take care of things." Anne paused.

"And?" promoted Jennifer.

"I said I'd try."

"I suppose it will hit me at some point, but right now, I can't say I feel much of anything."

"Me either," her twin replied. "Things are dreadful at work. We've lost a couple of staff..." She paused. "The lawlessness and panic the pandemic has caused is scary. Society as we knew it is breaking down. I've been working twelve-hour days, six days a week. If it wasn't for Jim's visits on my day off, I don't know how I'd get through it."

"How is Jim?"

"He had the flu a week ago. Gave me a bit of a scare. He's fine, or so he says. He'll be here in a couple of days. It can't come fast enough."

"You really love him, don't you?" Jennifer felt her words sounded a little hollow, but her emotions and senses were dulled from exhaustion; she didn't have the energy to muster much enthusiasm.

Anne didn't seem to notice. "I do love him. I can't believe I'm saying those words. There's no way I could cope right now without his support."

"I'm glad you're not alone. I worry about you."

"How are *you* holding up? It can't be easy for you," Anne asked, changing the subject.

"It's horrible." As soon as the words were out of her mouth Jennifer fought to control her emotions. It was the first time she'd admitted it out loud, that what she had to do each day was sad and exhausting and awful. The word "horrible" covered it—the emotional drain, the physical demands, the mental stress and the constant deaths.

"History repeats itself," Anne said pragmatically. "We were overdue for a pandemic. Until you go through it though, it's just a few pages in a history book. Living it is quite something else."

"True," Jennifer responded. "I can't get away to get up north to see Mom, I just can't. Did she say anything about a funeral?"

"It's done," Anne said. "He died last week. There was no funeral. She had him cremated. There's too much snow to bury him now, so she'll bury him in the spring."

A long, deep sigh emanated from the core of her being. "How like her not to tell us. Sounds like you gave her the best advice you could. At some point, when this is over, I'll see if I can't get away for a few days. I suppose I should. Anyway, I gotta get to bed, I'm exhausted. Thanks for letting me know."

"Yeah. Take care of yourself."

"You too." Jennifer tapped off and dropped her phone onto the end table. She dragged herself to her feet and started the shower. The hot water washed away any feelings of the day, including those for her mother and father. She was just too tired to feel much of anything.

10

Jennifer woke the next morning as exhausted as she had been when she fell into bed. She forced herself downstairs to her office, oblivious to the sunshine sparkling on the snow in the early morning light.

She started the day with the messages waiting on her phone. She called the arena, the night shift supervisor said he'd called in two people to cover the morning shift, two directors had the flu. Relieved the day shift was taken care of, she checked the rest of the messages. Elaine's husband had called to say Elaine wouldn't be in, and Brent had left a message the night before asking her to call. Glancing at the time, she dialed his home number.

"Hi, Brent." She didn't give him her usual cheery greeting. He did not respond with anything cheery, either.

"Hi, Jennifer. Getting straight to the point, I'm going to have to take some time off. I can't keep going."

"Understood. You honoured our pact. Take as long as you need and don't even think about coming back until you're ready. OK?"

"OK. I do feel like I'm letting you guys down."

"Don't," she said firmly. "Don't go there. This is about you and what you need. I mean it, take all the time you feel is necessary."

"Thanks. I'll call when I'm ready to come back."

After a brief goodbye, they disconnected. She hadn't even thought to ask Brent how Julie and the girls were. Leaning back in her chair, Jennifer realized she hadn't recognized the warning signs indicating that Brent was exhausted and burned out. Someone had mentioned to her Brent had been quiet lately. Was it Marcia or Jeff? She couldn't remember.

She heard Roger come in and make a coffee. She did not get up to greet him, just continued to sit in her chair, staring at her computer screen, nothing registering.

Someone else entered the workroom and this time she took notice. She leaned over and looked out her open door. Jeff sat at his workstation with a young woman Jennifer hadn't seen before. Pulling herself to her feet, she went to see him.

"Jeff. How are you?" He looked up at her and smiled.

"I'm OK. This is Laura. She's going to help us hire and coordinate the transfer teams. I asked Lucas to supervise the teams. He has a few weeks' experience. We need more workers. We aren't getting applicants like we used to. Laura is going to go back through the old interview lists and see if she can't hire some of the ones we initially rejected."

Laura looked up at Jennifer and smiled. "Hello, Ms. Spencer."

"Glad you're here."

"I'm happy to help."

"I'll let you get to it." Jennifer turned at her office door to say something to Jeff but stopped herself. He and Laura were once again deep in conversation. Restless, she sought out Roger in the lounge. He was leafing through some files, with more piled on the table beside him.

"Hi, Roger."

"Hi, Jennifer. Is Elaine coming in today?"

"No."

"Marcia?"

"I think so. Why?"

"All these files need to be put into the computer. I need burial permits and cremation certificates and someone has to go to the crematorium. Elaine usually takes care of those details for me."

"I'll do it for you," Jennifer said. "What needs to be done first?"

"I need cremation certificate for these two." He handed her the files. "I put notes on the outside of these." He handed her a small pile. "Oh, there is a lady coming in this morning who asked for you specifically. She said something about her husband being a police Lieutenant."

"Yes. I'll see her. Did she say what time?"

"I wrote it down here somewhere. He fumbled through the remaining pages in front of him. Jennifer could feel her impatience rise.

"Can't seem to find it right now. I'll let you know."

Without a word she went to the counter and made herself a coffee. She was angry and frustrated with the old director and didn't trust herself to speak. He made work for them by not learning to input and use a computer or cell phone. He couldn't drive to the crematorium or city hall or anywhere for that matter. She picked up her coffee and went to her office, closing the door, hoping to get some work done. She had emails to catch up on.

Dully, she stared at her computer, barely noticing she'd been sipping her coffee, her mind frozen. She flipped through a couple of the folders Roger had given her, pushing them aside after scanning them.

An email alert caught her attention and she idly clicked on it. At first it didn't register. It was from Dr. Bolton at the Public Health Unit, with a cc to Mr. Whitney, notifying them the flu had claimed Sarah's life. He named her replacement but Jennifer didn't finish reading it. The words were meaningless. Sarah, an expert in infectious disease, a vital part of the health care team had died from the very thing she worked so hard to prevent and control. Jennifer closed her eyes and thought about Sarah and how hard she had worked to achieve her goals.

A tap on the door pulled her out of her shock as Marcia poked her head around the corner.

"Roger says you have some certificates to pick up. Should I do it?"

"Do you have time?"

"I'll make time. Are you OK? You look awfully pale." Marcia closed the door behind her and sat down in a chair across from the desk.

"Something's wrong. I just know it. What is it?"

"It's everything. Sarah is dead, my dad died, Elaine is off sick, Brent has had to take some time off, the arena staffing is getting to be problematic—"

"Whoa. Slow down. Your dad died? When?"

Jennifer shrugged her indifference. "Last week sometime."

"Oh Jen, I'm sorry. I know you weren't close, but it's still your dad. Is your mom OK?"

"Anne says she wants us to go up north to help her. I don't think that's going to happen. Neither of us can get away. She has a lawyer to help with all that anyway."

Marcia studied her quietly. "Still, it's hard for you. And to lose Sarah, she was your go-to at the Health Unit."

"Yeah."

"At least Brent has the sense to know when it's time to take a break," Marcia said. "I wish Ryan could. He's going to burn out, too."

"That reminds me. The Lieutenant's wife will be in sometime today."

"Roger just mentioned it. He told me to tell you she'll be in at ten, which is why I offered to do the running around."

"Take Roger with you, or call in someone from Williams. It's safer."

"All right." As she exited the office, Marcia turned back to Jennifer and looked at her intensely. She opened her mouth to say something, caught herself, and then closed the door quietly behind her.

Turning to her computer again, Jennifer forced herself to focus on the rest of the emails. Three staff members were unable to do their upcoming shifts at the arena and needed to be replaced. She started making calls, running down the list. Almost twenty calls later she had the shifts covered, at least until someone else called in sick. It was never-ending.

Another tap at the door made her stiffen. She just wanted to be left alone.

"Come in," she responded, aware from her mood she needed to sound neutral and not let her irritation show.

Peter and Jordan pushed the door open and entered.

"Hi, Jennifer," said Peter brightly. "Brent's off. He called to say he'd let us know when he'd be back. Gordon asked me to tell you we have six calls today. Is there someone you can send over? Jordan and I have the night shift, but we can help out for the rest of the day."

"First, how's the baby? How's Angel?" She couldn't help but smile as Peter's face lit up. The new baby was the only bright spot in her crappy morning.

"They're great. She is such a doll. She slept six hours last night."

Glancing at her computer to check the time, Jennifer noticed it was nearly 10:00 a.m. The Lieutenant's wife would be there in a few minutes.

"Sit down you two," she said. Jordan looked at her quizzically but obeyed. Leaning forward slightly she folded her hands and looked from one to the other solemn face.

"I think it's time for both of you to start making arrangements, under Gordon's supervision, of course." Peter and Jordan exchanged glances and she could detect a flash of interest pass between them. They kept their faces solemn.

"We haven't done any at school yet, but I think we can," Peter said. Jordan nodded his affirmation.

"I'll call Gordon and let him know. It's not part of the regulations under the Act, we all know that, but we no longer have choices. I trust you both implicitly." She ran her hand through her hair, there was something else she was planning on asking them. It took her a few seconds to remember.

"There is one more thing. Staffing at the arena is becoming a problem. Do either of you feel ready to work alone if necessary, under the supervision of one of the directors there?"

Jordan exhaled and shook his head no. Peter just looked thoughtful and took his time answering.

"We'll do what has to be done."

Jordan looked at his friend and back at Jennifer.

"All right."

"OK, you two. Thank you. Remember what you've been taught, don't deviate from protective measures, and if you get run down or tired, tell me. You can't let yourself get exhausted. Deal?"

"Deal," responded Peter as the two of them rose.

"Oh, one more thing. Would one of you team up with Marcia for an hour or so?"

"Sure, I will," responded Jordan as the two of them left her office. The door didn't have time to shut and Roger was waiting to speak to her.

"The Lieutenant's wife, Mrs. Turcott, is here. I put her in the front office."

"Thanks." Jennifer picked up a blank file, noting she needed to stock up on forms. She hadn't had the time to fill out the preliminary details. She'd barely started her email list and there were still calls waiting on her phone she hadn't looked at. *And* she needed to get to the arena at some point to assess the call volume.

Once again, the was day slipping away from her. She stood, started for the door, stopped to think for a few seconds and turned back to her desk. Picking up the landline she called Desta at Williams. It took a few rings before the secretary answered.

"Desta, may I forward our calls to you for about an hour?" *No time for hi, how are you, just work, just like Anne.*

"Of course," Desta responded.

"Thanks." She hung up, forwarded the line, and started toward the front office. A young couple stood in the lobby, glancing around, looking uncomfortable.

"Have you been looked after?" They looked at her dully and shook their heads no.

"I'm sorry. Let me get someone for you. I'm Jennifer, one of the directors here. Please, take a seat." She didn't wait for a response, she immediately sought out Roger, finding him in the front suite with a family, the door closed. She didn't interrupt. There was no sign of Marcia and she realized her friend had left to do a crematorium run with Jordan.

Walking back to the lobby, she asked the young couple if they would mind waiting in the lounge or come back in about an hour. She felt terrible as they said they would wait, and followed her to the lounge. Sure, they were walk-ins but she had a policy of not keeping people waiting too long. Once they were settled she went to the office where she found a well-dressed, immaculately presented woman in her late fifty's sitting primly in one of the wingback chairs.

"Sorry to keep you, Mrs. Turcott," she said, forcing her voice to be measured and calm.

"Yes, well, I did have an appointment and I was here on time," came the curt response. *Let it go Jennifer. Let it go.*

Taking a seat behind the desk, she opened the folder and picked up her pen. "I'm sorry about your husband. Detective Sergeant Gillespie informed me about his death." She watched as Mrs. Turcott knotted and twisted a linen handkerchief in her gloved hands.

"Did he also tell you my husband, who served on the force for thirty-eight years, has been refused a police funeral? Did he?"

Jennifer could feel the rage radiating from this grieving woman, almost matching her own. She knew Ryan had made it clear to Mrs. Turcott the police funeral would be held at a later date.

"The District Health Unit made the decision, Mrs. Turcott. It doesn't mean the police funeral won't be held, it just means it will be delayed until the pandemic passes."

"That's just nonsense. I called the health unit, but they did not even give me the courtesy of a return call. I intend to take this matter to our member of provincial parliament. I left a message for him. I'm sure *he* will return the call."

"Did you speak with his assistant?" asked Jennifer as she tried to process what she perceived as the women's lack of insight into the severity of the pandemic and the effect it was having on services.

"No, it went to voice mail. But I'm sure he'll call. My husband certainly saw him at enough regional functions. Of course, he'll call." Her hands twisted the handkerchief faster and tighter. Her increase in agitation was not lost on Jennifer.

"Perhaps we should get some of the details out of the way. When he calls, we will be ready." She didn't tell her the MPP would probably not be calling. She had read in the news his office was on skeleton staff. Even the MPP could not override the health official in this situation. Mrs. Turcott obviously needed to feel she had some control.

"Fine," was her clipped response. Jennifer worked through the information carefully. The Turcotts had no children. Once the preliminaries were out of the way, she put her pen down and sat back.

"In the event there could be a delay, I can assure you your husband will be placed in a vault at the cemetery until the ceremony."

"I told you, there will be no delay! This will get done. The service will be on Monday."

Jennifer rose slowly so she would not further annoy the upset woman. Mrs. Turcott was probably scared and lost, she didn't need her funeral director showing any irritation.

"Perhaps we should select a suitable casket for the Lieutenant," she said kindly. Mrs. Turcott's shoulder's relaxed and the tight lines around her mouth softened.

"Of course," she rose and Jennifer noted the expensive handbag and shoes and suit.

In the selection room Mrs. Turcott demanded to see the real version of the walnut casket on the interactive display. There was one in stock, at Williams. No one was free to bring it over though.

"I will take you over to Williams Funeral Home so you can see if the casket you have selected meets your requirements. If you wouldn't mind taking a seat in the lounge, I will get the car ready."

She had completely forgot about the young couple, who were still waiting as Mrs. Turcott followed her into the lounge. Where was Roger? What was keeping Marcia?

"I'll make a few calls," she said as Mrs. Turcott took a seat.

"A few? There's one casket, the one I chose for my husband, why a few?"

Jennifer's frustration peaked—because of herself and her client, mostly her client.

"Correct, sorry. I'll be right back." She went into her office, scowling as soon as she turned her back on the annoying Mrs. Turcott and checked the supply list for the two funeral homes on her computer. Jennifer called Desta.

"Hi, Desta, me again. I'm bringing a lady over to view the walnut casket. It's showing as in stock. Do you have time to double check for me?"

"Sure, I'll put you on hold. Gordon and Peter are busy. Jordan's still with Marcia, so I'll run downstairs and look."

While on hold, she texted Marcia who did not get back her immediately. "She must be driving," she muttered to herself. Jennifer drummed her fingers on her desk and clicked on her emails. The few that had been waiting earlier in the day had grown to a long list. She scanned them, not taking in much information, her mind wandering, as she waited for Desta to return.

"Jennifer? Is it blackish wood with a white interior? Gold handles?"

"It is."

"I'll see if I can get it pulled out and put in our selection room for you. When are you coming?"

"Now. Thanks, Desta."

Jennifer went through the workroom and out into the prep room hallway in order to avoid the lounge. She felt guilty about keeping the young couple waiting and she needed to see when Roger would be free.

He was still with the family he'd been with earlier. Hesitating briefly, she broke her rule of not interrupting a director during arrangements and tapped gently on the door.

"What is it?" As he opened the door, Roger didn't disguise his annoyance.

"We have a family in the lounge waiting to be seen. I have to take Mrs. Turcott over to Williams. How much longer do you think you'll be?"

"I will be done when I'm done," he said. "I don't appreciate the interruption." Without another word, he closed the door in her face. His behaviour stunned her. Shaking her head, she pulled her phone out and dialed Marcia, walking outside to the garage at the back of the lot as it rang. Ignoring the cold, she continued to let it ring until Marcia answered it.

"What's up?" Marcia said cheerfully. "Sorry it took so long, had to pull over."

"Roger is with a family. I am taking Mrs. Turcott over to Williams to look at a casket, they can't bring it over and we have a young couple who have been waiting for a while. What's your ETA?"

"Ten minutes?" suggested Marcia. "I've done city hall, just going to Williams to drop Jordan off. I'll take care of it."

"Thank you." Jennifer couldn't hide her relief.

"It's weird out here," Marcia said. "The streets are practically deserted, there's garbage all over the place. I hadn't noticed it being this bad before. I just called Ryan, someone tried to flag me down, but I didn't dare stop. Oh, there it is. He sent a squad car to follow me back to the funeral home. I'll be there shortly." Jennifer could hear her exhale with relief.

"I'm sorry, Marcia. We should always be in pairs. We won't do it again, even for short distances, I promise."

"No, we won't." Her friend laughed with relief. "Ryan read me the riot act. Really though, Jen, it's not safe out here. Who would've thought such a normally pleasant drive could be so scary?"

"I'm just glad you're OK. I'll let the young couple know. I haven't had time to get any files together or input anything. I don't even have their names. Sorry."

"No worries. We'll get it done." As Marcia disconnected Jennifer pulled up the garage door and hit the car starter and locks. *What would I do without her? She's kept me sane.* Jennifer pulled the car up to the portico and entered the funeral home. The lounge was silent. Mrs. Turcott turned sideways in her chair, away from the young couple.

"Marcia will be with you in about ten minutes," she said to the young couple. They nodded.

"Mrs. Turcott?"

Without a word, Mrs. Turcott retrieved her coat and followed her to the car. Jennifer started to reach for the front passenger door handle, then changed her mind. She opened the door to the back seat and chauffeured the woman to Williams. Not a word was exchanged between them.

Two blocks from Williams, Jennifer stopped at a red light. She hadn't been paying attention to her surroundings, she was so preoccupied. Seemingly out of nowhere, a group of young men surrounded the car and pounded on the doors and windows. One stood in front of the vehicle to prevent her from moving forward.

Terror seized her. She sat frozen, her hands gripping the steering wheel. She was unable to think or react to the danger. The group of men rocked the car, their faces pressed up to the windows, yelling and demanding money. Jennifer was vaguely aware Mrs. Turcott had let her window down. She heard a scream from one of the men, just as quickly followed by a second scream.

"GO!" yelled Mrs. Turcott. Jennifer's foot hit the gas pedal and the young man blocking the front of the car dove to the side. She felt and heard a sickening thump as the car hit him. Tires spinning, heart pounding, she sped the remaining two blocks to Williams Funeral Home. This time, it was Mrs. Turcott who opened the door for a shaken Jennifer. She took the keys from her hand and, locking the car doors, steered her inside the building.

"What happened?" Desta took one look at Jennifer's ghostly face, then at Mrs. Turcott.

"I think this young lady could use some tea," responded Mrs. Turcott pragmatically. "I need to call the station and let them know they may have to dispatch an ambulance and officers." She pulled out her phone and followed Desta and Jennifer downstairs, calmly giving the 911 operator the details.

Once Jennifer had a few swallows of tea and her heart had slowed its pounding, she glanced over at Mrs. Turcott with new-found respect. With not a hair out of place, Mrs. Turcott serenely sipped her tea.

"What happened? How did you get them to stop?"

"Easy, my dear. The Lieutenant gave me some bear spray and told me to carry it at all times. He explained such things could happen during the pandemic. He wanted me safe. As usual, he was right. I opened my purse, took out my wallet, which distracted them, and slipped the spray into my right hand. I unrolled the window and nailed two of them." She smiled a soft smile, more to herself than to Jennifer and Desta.

Staring at the older woman, feeling more than a little ashamed of herself, Jennifer realized she'd seriously misjudged Mrs. Turcott. But bear spray? It was likely pepper spray, which made it illegal to carry in Ontario. It didn't matter, they were safe. The Lieutenant did what he needed to protect his wife. She and Desta exchanged surprised glances at Mrs. Turcott's calmness.

"Thank you. I panicked. You got us out of a tough situation."

With a slight incline of her head, Mrs. Turcott acknowledged the praise. Putting her cup down, she straightened in the chair. "Shall we?"

Desta led them to the selection room where she'd prepared the casket. Mrs. Turcott studied it intensely. Jennifer could see her struggling to hold back the tears.

"That's the one." She linked her arm in Jennifer's and walked to the bottom of the stairs. "I think we should call for an escort, don't you dear? I've had enough stress for one day." One call from Mrs. Turcott and within ten minutes they had a squad car follow them back to the funeral home.

The officer waited while Mrs. Turcott gave Jennifer a sincere hug, got into her vehicle, and followed the squad car out of the lot. Shaking her head in disbelief, Jennifer went inside and called the arena. The sergeant informed her he would be able to send someone in an hour. She returned the car to the garage and vowed not to take it out again.

Marcia was with the young couple, the door to the suite closed. Roger was still with his family. Annoyed with his dawdling, Jennifer thought better of confronting him when he was finished. They really did need all the help they could get. She shouldn't pick a fight with him. He was a big help, freeing her to do her job at the arena.

Jennifer trudged upstairs to eat lunch and check on Grimsby. The stairs got harder to climb as her fatigue increased. She just wanted to lie down on the couch and nap. Instead, she used the time to check emails while eating. There were more cancellations for the evening shift and a message from Jeff letting her know he wasn't feeling well. He assured her that the shifts were covered and that Laura and Lucas were working well together.

Jennifer dialed Elaine's number to see how she was feeling. There was no answer. *She's probably sleeping. I'll try later.* Pushing the phone away, she finished her lunch before going downstairs to wait for the military driver.

11

On her way to the arena, Jennifer's phone rang. Gordon's name showed on the display. It dawned on her as she answered it that she'd forgotten to call him.

"Peter tells me he and Jordan are doing an evening shift at the arena. You forgot to let me know. I need them here." He made no attempt to hide his annoyance.

"Gordon, I'm sorry. Time got away from me. Perhaps I can come in for a few hours tonight and help you." It was the last thing she wanted to do.

"Fine. Next time, just tell me. It's hard enough with Brent and Jeff gone." He hung up.

Leaning her head back in the seat, she closed her eyes. First Roger, now Gordon. Jeff and Elaine were off sick and Brent was taking a mental health break. It felt like she was losing control as everyone pulled her in too many directions, doing the work of three people. The driver cleared the gate at the arena and she attempted to shake off the fatigue.

Her first stop was to check on the prep room team. She noticed the supervisor working at a prep table. He informed her one of the staff had gone home.

"We were only two people short for tonight," she said to him. "It had been four, but I made a decision to have our apprentices work without direct supervision. We just can't keep up to the staffing demands, there are too many directors off with influenza."

"Why didn't you let me know earlier? I haven't had dinner with my family for days. I told my wife I wouldn't be home because I was going to cover part of a shift."

"I'm sorry, I should have emailed it out. I managed to round up four. With Peter and Jordon coming in, we can cancel two. You can leave on time."

He looked at her, exasperated. "Fine, I'll call my wife." She didn't respond to his mood and he shook his head. "I'm sorry, Jennifer. I didn't mean to snap at you. I just heard one of our guys from the western part of the region died last night. I met him a few times. He had a wife and a couple of teenagers." He looked up at her. "Remember him? Tony, the

Italian guy?" She vaguely pictured a dark-haired pleasant man with an Italian accent.

"I do. How awful."

He abruptly changed the subject. "Have you been to the ice yet?" referring to the arena surface.

"No."

"Brace yourself," was his short comment as he turned back to his work.

"Thanks." As she left the room her anxiety mounted. Walking past the family room, she noticed Chaplain Regina and Chaplain Clive talking to family members. People were standing outside the door waiting their turn.

Looking straight ahead, Jennifer walked into the arena. She thought she'd be ready for an overflow situation, she and Captain Barry had talked about it, but she wasn't.

A tiny cry escaped her lips. The entire surface of the ice was full. Several military personnel walked among the bodies, checking tags. She could feel the blast of cold air from the large doors at the end of the arena and the beeping of a transport truck as it backed up.

"There you are." Captain Barry came up behind her. She turned quickly to him. Looking into each other's eyes, unspoken words between them showed their shock and concern. He steered her to the front row of the bleachers and they sat down.

The Captain ran his hand through his hair before asking, "Can you help us? We can't keep up. Registration is behind, families just keep coming in. We're doing our best, but it's getting out of hand. The coroner hasn't been in yet. We have several dozen more bodies in the truck that haven't been assigned numbers. The death certificates are piling up on the table over there." He inclined his head in the direction of the family room. "People are desperate to find their family members and we've kept them waiting for hours."

"Are you able to get more staff?"

"No. The police need help on the streets. We won't be getting help anytime soon, if at all."

She glanced at her watch. "I have four hours, if it helps. My funeral homes are short-staffed, I have to get back."

"Whatever time you have would be appreciated," he responded quietly. "Thank you." She remembered Dr. Bolton talking about a shortage of coroner's and registrars. Now there was a shortage of military staff.

She followed Captain Barry to the registration table, gowned and masked, sat down and started to match death certificates to tags, getting up to walk the ice surface to confirm the details every three bodies. Bending down, unzipping pouches and checking bands against tags and certificates took time.

She tried not to look at faces, but she couldn't help it. Distraught families cried around her, the distraction of their grief making her task harder. The cold ice surface caused a chill to creep through her body. Her feet and hands grew numb.

The four hours passed quickly. She was finishing her last trip to the ice surface when a name caught her attention. Heart pounding, she unzipped the pouch. It was Victoria Patterson's father.

She stared at him, reeling from the shock. Checking the date, she noted he had died two days before. She zipped the pouch and immediately went to the desk and pulled the medical certificate. Cause of death, cancer. *Mr. Patterson looked so drawn and thin when his wife died.*

Why had Victoria not claimed her father's body? Jennifer struggled to process the information when Captain Barry approached with the coroner, who immediately sat and started scribbling his initials on the certificates she'd piled on the desk.

"I confirmed sixty-three deaths," she said to the coroner. *Sixty-three too many. Why is Mr. Patterson still here? Where is Victoria?* She vaguely noted the coroner's exhaustion.

"Thanks Ms. Spencer. I think from now on I'll appoint you or one of your staff to alleviate my tasks here. I can't keep up, there's no one left to replace me and I'm needed at the hospitals. At least I can sign the death certificates there. I have several nurses taking care of the prison, jails and nursing homes for me." He took the tally sheet from her and without a word, left the arena.

Captain Barry had not spoken.

"How are we going to keep up?" she asked him, trying to hold the desperation from her voice. "We're short-staffed as it is."

"We can only do our best," he replied.

"I have to go. I need to be two other places right now *and* ensure there's enough staff for the midnight shift."

With no time to spare, she had the driver drop her at Williams. Desta was at her desk inputting information. Several families waited in the lobby.

"Have you eaten yet?" Jennifer asked her.

"I had my husband drop off some sandwiches. There are no take-out places nearby, not anymore.

The boys have been fed." She was referring to Jordan, Peter and Gordon. "Did you eat?" She looked at Jennifer, concerned.

"Yes," Jennifer lied. "At the arena." She hung up her coat and for the next six hours, didn't stop to think about what came next as she put her mind to the many tasks awaiting her.

Exhausted, she waited for Gordon to lock the funeral home and drive her home. They were both too tired to discuss their day, or pending duties, so they rode in silence. Thanking him, she unlocked the funeral home door, vacillating between going upstairs or to the office.

She quickly checked the files on Elaine's desk, noting sadly the young couple Marcia saw had lost their little boy. Ignoring the rest of the files, on legs that felt like lead, she trudged up the stairs to her apartment pulling herself up using the railing. Halfway up, she remembered she had planned to call Victoria Patterson to see how she was. She turned to go downstairs. *Maybe she is planning to use another funeral home. If I call her, it'll look like I'm asking her to come here. On the other hand, maybe she's ill.*

Victoria was on her own now, her parents and brother gone in a matter of weeks. It would be overwhelming for anyone, and Jennifer knew she had to reach out to her. Pulling the file up on the computer she tried Victoria's cell phone. Her voicemail was full. She tried the Patterson house, no answer. She thought back to the last time she had seen Victoria. It had been weeks ago, at the grocery store. Jennifer, aware of the grief load the young woman carried, found she was managing the death of her mother and brother, at least on the surface, as expected. *Something just doesn't add up. I'll try reaching her tomorrow. I let her down, I keep making promises to connect with her and then forget.*

Overwhelmed with exhaustion, Jennifer went upstairs, took a quick shower, made sure Grimsby was fed, and fell into bed. Her dreams were of rows and rows of white body bags and snow falling on them, covering them. She tried to dig them out so she could identify them, to no avail.

Waking the next morning she was nauseous and edgy. She drank half her coffee and, finding it made her queasy, she dumped the rest down the sink. Mentally she was exhausted. *I have to find Victoria.* She called for her military driver, looked up the address for the Patterson home and when he pulled up, asked him to help her with a wellness check and gave him the address.

Pulling up to the Patterson home she was surprised at the size of the property and house. She knew Mr. Patterson was, or rather, had been, a successful businessman. Clearly, she had not been aware from her time with the family just how wealthy they were. There were no cars in the driveway, the four garage doors were closed. She asked her driver to wait while she rang the doorbell.

As Jennifer walked from the car to the front stoop, the knot in her stomach tightened with every step. There was no answer. She looked around, knocked, then blocking the driver's view, she tried the door knob with her gloved hand. It was unlocked.

Impulsively, she pushed the door open and entered to an eerie silence. A cat, meowing plaintively, brushed up against her then ran outside.

"Hello? Is anyone home?" she called, her heart thumping, partly with unease at her unauthorized entry and partly with fear.

No response.

She took a few steps into the foyer. She could see a large kitchen off to her right. It looked as if someone had been baking and left in a hurry. Victoria had mentioned she was picking up something for her baking. She backed slowly out the house and closed the door. *I should have checked to see if Mr. Patterson died at home and who the transfer team was. Maybe they know what happened.* Jennifer hurried back to the car.

At the arena she thanked the driver and went immediately to the ice surface, doing her best not to look at the rows and rows of bodies. A corporal looked up for the stacks of certificates and papers as she approached.

"Hi," she said pleasantly, doing her best to hide her anxiety. "Can you tell me if anyone from the Patterson family has been in to claim the body?"

He looked the alphabetized certificates and pulled the file.

"Nope," he said, shaking his head.

"Who did the transfer?"

"Umm, can't read the signature. Does that look like Manuel to you? He turned the file to her to show her.

"I think so. Thanks." As she walked away from the table she called Jeff's replacement, Lucas, who answered quickly.

"Hi Jennifer."

"How is it going?"

"Busy. Too busy. The teams are exhausted. But no more so than your teams, I suppose."

"It's hard on everyone," she responded. "Do you have a Manuel on your team?"

"Ya, he works nights. Good worker. Why?"

"I have a question for him. Could you give him my cellphone number and have him call me? It's important."

"Sure. Is something wrong?"

"No, no, he did nothing wrong. I just need to clarify something with him about a transfer he did."

"I'll text him now, he might be sleeping. If you don't hear from him by later tonight, here's his number."

Jennifer typed the number into her contacts and as Jeff disconnected she added Manuel's name. *Please don't let him be sleeping. Somethings wrong, I just know it. Victoria would not just disappear.*

Her phone rang, but it wasn't Manuel. The rest of the day passed in a blur of work. She didn't have time to eat or check the time. There was just too much to do.

Manuel did call later that evening. He didn't recall the specifics of the transfer until she described the Patterson house.

"Oh yeah, that one. Apparently, whoever called said the front door was open and to go to the upstairs master bedroom. There was no one else there, just the dead guy. We took him to the arena."

"Was it a man or woman who called?"

"Dunno. We were dispatched from whoever was on the transfer desk. I don't even remember who that was. You'll have to check with them."

Trying to keep the frustration out of her voice, Jennifer thanked Manuel and called Lucas.

"Hi, Lucas. Thanks for having Manuel get back to me. Do you do much dispatching or does it come from the hospital?"

"Hospital, arena, usually a corporal on the desk, sometimes a funeral home. I take the messages and dispatch the teams."

I should have remembered that. I wasted a day trying to find out and the answer may have been here all the time.

"Thanks." She tapped off and went to the Sergeant's desk at the front of the arena.

She stood impatiently while the information was retrieved.

"Hospice worker. No name," came the response to her query.

"Do you have the number for the Hospice Team?" The Sergeant scribbled it down for her and she dialled it as she walked away.

Identifying herself and the reason for her call, the hospice team member put her on hold while they checked and she paced.

"That's interesting. Mr. Patterson was on our visitation list, but we have no record of his death. When did he die?"

"A couple of days ago," she responded.

"Then we missed something. He was getting daily visits from the nurse. She should have notified us. So many of our staff are off with illness…" Her voice trailed off. "MaryLou was looking after him. She has been off sick for a week. Maybe she left the meds with Mr. Patterson's daughter, Victoria. Did you ask her?"

Jennifer's fear heightened. "I'll check with her. Thanks for your help." She tapped off and took a deep breath. There was no Victoria to check with.

She called DS Sue Ziegler at the police station. Her line rang for a while before someone else picked it up. She gave the officer the details.

"What did you say your name was again?" the constable asked.

She gritted her teeth in frustration before she relaxed her jaw, took a breath and replied, "Jennifer Spencer."

"So, you are reporting a missing person?"

"Essentially, yes."

"Well, Ms. Spencer, we are backed up with cases. I will pass this on to the missing person's department and I'll make sure Detective Sergeant Ziegler gets your message. It's been over a few days you said?"

"Yes." *The nurse would have reported Victoria missing, or Mr. Patterson would have.*

"Perhaps Ms. Patterson is out of town. People are hard to find these days. They are trying to get away from this flu. She could be anywhere. Keep trying her cell phone and if you don't hear from her by next week, call us again. In the meantime, *if* we have time, we will run a quick check to see if anyone else has reported her missing. Will that be all Ms. Spencer?"

"Yes, thank you." She tapped off in frustration. *Now what? Victoria could be in trouble.* John. John would help. Shaking, she tapped his number. He answered immediately.

"Jennifer, is everything alright?"

Relief swept over her. John would take care of it. She found a quiet place to sit as she gave him the details. He listened intensely, stopping only to ask a question or to clarify something. Some questions she couldn't answer and she told John she'd have to check her file at the funeral home.

"I have Victoria's phone number, I'll get my team on it right away. Jim can check to see when her cell phone was last used. Call me when you get the rest of the information." He paused. "Actually, never mind. I can send a security team to the Patterson house. You gave me the street name, that should be enough."

"Thank you, John. Are you doing well?"

"I'm fine. You sound tired."

His voice was gentle and reflected his concern. Suddenly she felt the urge to cry. She wasn't tired, she was exhausted and overwhelmed. Closing her eyes, she pictured John in his red sweater Christmas night and his delight when she accepted the pen. A tear trickled down her cheek as she inhaled a deep, controlled breath and composed herself.

"I'm in survival mode." *Why did I say that? John is busy too, he doesn't need to know I've almost reached my limit.* She continued quickly. "I'm worried about Victoria. With the gangs roaming, maybe something happened to her, maybe she was mugged. Maybe she's sick somewhere and can't get help. The police office I spoke to kind of brushed it off."

"Leave it with me. You focus on your needs. We got this."

"Thanks. I really appreciate it."

He chuckled. "It's my job. You do seem to have a knack for getting into situations out of your league. I'll keep you posted. Bye."

"Bye," she responded softly. A tiny smile played at the corners of her mouth as he disconnected. He was right, she did seem to need "backup" from time to time. This time, though, it was for Victoria. The relief at John's willingness to find the girl lightened her mood.

The days were a blur as Jennifer pushed herself to stay on top of the massive workload. She pulled Laura from transfers, asked her to appoint her replacement and put her on the front desk of the funeral home. Desta was happy to have the extra help. Laura proved to be a quick study—she had almost completed her BA in commerce before the pandemic. With Roger and Marcia's help, she fell comfortably into the role of receptionist and office manager.

Trying to sustain herself on three to four hours of sleep a night wasn't working for Jennifer. Increasing irritability was hard to keep at bay. She had moments of nausea and lightheadedness. On day five of Brent's absence, standing in her kitchen she bent down to pick up Grimsby's dish and fainted, waking up on the floor twenty minutes later. Unhurt, she pulled herself up by grabbing the edge of the counter, her head swimming. Stumbling to her room, she fell onto the bed and into a deep sleep, awaking into bright sunshine and a ringing phone.

Pulling her phone from her pocket she answered it, her mouth pasty and dry, her eyes heavy and gritty.

"Hello, Jen. It's Sandy." Elaine's husband. Jennifer sat on the edge of her bed, doing her best to focus.

"I know it's early," he started to say before he stopped, choking back a sob. A prickle of fear ran through her.

"I'm up," she lied. It happened all too easily these days.

"Elaine died last night."

The air felt as if it had been sucked out of the room. Struggling to comprehend what she'd just heard, she was aware Sandy was asking if he could come in at 9:00 a.m.

Numb with shock, she replied, "Yes." The conversation ended with her answer, neither of them able to continue. Sandy disconnected.

Dropping the phone on the bed, a primal wail rose from deep inside her. Wrapping her arms tightly around herself, she wept like she had never wept before. Grimsby moved beside his mistress and pressed into her, his eyes wide, frightened by the sounds she made.

Finally spent, she scooped him into her arms and buried her wet face in his fur. Glancing at her phone again, it showed 7:00 a.m. She'd have to wait to tell the staff. Nauseous and shaky from exhaustion, and numb with grief, she went through the motions of washing her face and combing her hair. She didn't have the energy to put on makeup. She changed to a clean suit and made herself a coffee, barely able to take a few sips before she vomited. An hour and a half passed before she was able to pick up her phone and call Marcia, still crying.

"I have some bad news."

She could hear Marcia take a deep breath as she prepared herself.

"Elaine…"

She couldn't finish the sentence, she broke into sobs.

"She's gone? No, please tell me it isn't true."

Jennifer barely heard herself ask Marcia to break the news to the rest of the staff. A badly shaken Marcia agreed. They disconnected, neither able to discuss it at that point in time.

Stiff and sore, Jennifer slowly went downstairs, gripping the handrail. She unlocked the front door and stood in the cold air, waiting for Elaine's husband.

Together they wept, sharing their grief before getting down to the business of arranging Elaine's funeral.

I can't say goodbye to the one person who felt most like a mother to me. First Aunt Jean, then Uncle Bill, now Elaine. It's too much. For a brief second, an image of her mother flashed through Jennifer's mind, she pushed it aside. Her mother had said she "needed" her and Anne. It would have to wait. She had no room for her mother's needs. People closer to her needed her help.

When Sandy had signed the necessary documentation and left, Jennifer found a quiet, subdued Marcia waiting for her in the lounge. Wordlessly the two of them hugged, tears running down their cheeks and onto each other's shoulders, as Roger looking on sympathetically.

"I'm sorry," he said sadly. "I liked Elaine. You girls will miss her."

Jennifer nodded affirmatively at him. "Thanks," she said brokenly, her sadness and grief making it hard for her to talk. Roger's tone surprised her, his voice didn't have its usual edge.

"Tea?" Marcia asked. Jennifer nodded.

"I got it." Roger stood up and went to the counter. He made tea for both women and placed it in front of them as they sat silent in their grief.

"I called Brent at home first, before I called his staff. Jeff's mom said she'd tell him. He's still in bed sick," said Marcia. "Peter was pretty shaken. Brent will be back at work this afternoon."

Raising her head, Jennifer looked at Marcia. "Is he *ready* to come back? He not just—"

Marcia nodded. "I asked him the same question. He said he was. He said he didn't think about work when he was off, just focused on his family. He said he needed to come back and support his staff." She looked pensive before she continued. "Desta took the news quite hard. She and Elaine were close."

Jennifer looked down at the floor. She had nothing to say, nothing more to ask. The funeral home would not be the same without Elaine. She was their backbone, the glue that held them all together. She'd been there for Jennifer since her early teens. Elaine was her strength when Aunt Jean and Uncle Bill died. Elaine was her surrogate mother, more of a mother to her than her own. Her chest ached with the pain of the loss and the grief washing over her.

Laura and Roger continued with the business of running the funeral home while Jennifer sat numbly in the lounge. It took several hours before Jennifer was ready to get back to work. She pushed herself to her feet and went into her office to check with the arena and send for the military driver.

Marcia would be riding in with her. She was working a shift-and-a-half while Jennifer helped with the documentation in the arena. With trembling hands, she prepared a file for Elaine, then tucked it into her briefcase to complete the work on it at the arena.

Marcia climbed into the military van behind Jennifer, both lost in their grief, too tired to chat. At the arena, they went different directions without a goodbye. Marcia was supervising the shift. Peter would be working the first, Jordan the second. Several other funeral directors were coming and going from the busy prep area. Jennifer wandered to the family room where several people chatted with

Chaplain Clive. He was focused on listening to an elderly gentleman, and did not notice her.

He looks exhausted. How can he keep up this insane pace? If anything happened to him… She wanted to tell him about Elaine. It would have to wait.

Wandering into the canteen, she picked up a muffin and coffee and went to the documentation table in the arena. She knew she shouldn't eat near all the bodies, but she just didn't care. The change of temperature slammed her, causing a violent shiver to run through her body.

She glanced up. Captain Barry was hard at work, sorting the piles of paperwork, the business end of death stacked around him. She tried not to look at the arena floor, but the smell and feel of death drew her eyes to the ice surface. Several of the transfer team walked down the rows of bodies and acknowledged her with a tiny wave. They didn't stop to talk. There was no time. Death demanded it all.

"Miss, Miss! Can you help me?" Someone came up behind her and grabbed her arm. She tried to jerk away, startled. She turned to see a middle-aged woman, her height, eyes wild with fear.

"I can't find him. I can't find my son. They said he was here. Can you help me?" The woman's grip was strong. Even through her coat Jennifer felt the intensity of it. She knew the determined mother wasn't going to let go until she got an answer.

"Come, let's check over here." She led the woman to the table where Captain Barry sat. The desperately grieving mother still clung to her until Jennifer gently removed her hand.

With a few leading questions and Captain Barry's assistance, they located the death certificate. Immediately Jennifer's eye was drawn to the secondary cause of death. The young man, in his early thirties, had Down's Syndrome.

"Let me get just a few more details from you, then I'll take you to him," Jennifer said. The woman nodded. Captain Barry reached over and pulled out the chair beside him for Jennifer. The woman took a seat across from them.

As she took the details for the death registration, Jennifer learned the woman's husband had died many years before, leaving her with a young, disabled son. Her son required heart surgery when he was a child but had eventually been able to attend school. As part of a work program, he cleaned tables at a diner. The customers, his mother said, loved him. Every day when he came home from work, he told her joyfully about his day.

"He never complained, he was always happy. Such a good boy." The mother's sobs filled the air in the arena. Automatically Jennifer pushed the tissue box close to her and glanced over at Captain Barry. He didn't notice her glance, he was watching the young man's mother, his face awash with empathy.

Jennifer's thoughts flashed back to a classmate she had in high school. She couldn't remember her real name, she knew her as "Missy." She too, had Down's Syndrome and though she struggled with academics, she was fairly high-functioning. Thinking back, Jennifer never heard her complain about anything either. Missy was always pleasant, even when teased by ignorant students. As a teenager she'd been indifferent to Missy's friendship overtures, and she felt a pang of guilt as she listened to the mother in front of her talk about her son's struggles and her pride in his successes.

When the mother's tears were temporarily spent, Jennifer rose, took her arm and walked her to her son, her head down as she silently guided her through the bodies. Jennifer didn't want to look around to see or feel the weight and impact of the pandemic's scourge as she led the way through the rows and rows of bodies. She stayed with the mother while she identified her son and continued to stand by as the woman said her goodbyes. Jennifer fixed her gaze at the top of the bleachers, willing herself not to let her emotions overwhelm her.

When the mother was ready, Jennifer led her to the arena door and returned quietly to her duties at the registration table, her mind on the details of Elaine's funeral. Hours later, she and Captain Barry caught up for the first time in days. It was a small victory, albeit a short one as she heard the sound of a transport truck backing up to the arena doors.

12

Exhausted, Marcia and Jennifer climbed into the military vehicle and sat in silence. It was nearly midnight and much of the day had been a blur for both of them. Leaning back in the seat and resting her head, Marcia sighed.

"Ryan has this weekend off. I think I'll take it off, too. It feels like this has gone on forever and it's never going to end."

Jennifer looked over to see a tear trickle down her friend's cheek. "It does." She had nothing productive to add or say.

Several blocks later Marcia opened her eyes and leaned forward as far as her seatbelt would allow.

"I need milk," she said to the driver. "Do you know if there are any convenience stores open at this hour?"

"Yep," he replied. "There's one not too far from here."

Most of the stores had shut down for the duration of the pandemic. Some were open only during the day as looting and a shortage of food and supplies caused them to close early. It was dangerous to be out at night.

The driver pulled up to the store and Marcia slid out, disappearing inside. He watched her closely through the window as she went to the back cooler. Several minutes passed and Jennifer, lost in a fog of fatigue, startled as he jumped out of the car.

"Stay here," he ordered, slamming the car door behind him. Jolting to her senses, she watched him run into the store and disappear down the aisle.

Sitting up taller, she could see him grab someone and pull them. She couldn't see Marcia through the shelves and Jennifer's heart started pounding. *Oh, no... not now. Not Marcia.* The clerk at the front counter was on the phone, gesturing wildly. Scanning frantically, Jennifer finally saw Marcia move into view. Seconds later another military vehicle pulled in and the occupant ran into the store, emerging less than a minute later with her friend. He opened the car door for her and helped her inside. He stood beside the car, his back to them.

"We got her," a breathless Marcia said.

Jennifer ignored her comment.

"Are you OK? Are you hurt?"

"I'm fine. It's Elizabeth who might need medical attention."

"What?" Jennifer's incredulous response sounded more like a squeak than a question.

"I decked her." Marcia was clearly pleased with herself. "I didn't think I had it in me to hit another human being." She turned sideways in the car to face Jennifer. "I've never done that to anyone before. I hate to say it, but it felt good to take the little brat down. She came at me for no reason."

A police car pulled into the lot, light's flashing. Two officers, in no hurry, walked into the store. Marcia turned back to the window and craned her neck to see what was going on.

"Darn, our 'bodyguard' is blocking my view," she muttered.

"Marcia!" Jennifer's tone got her friend's attention. "What happened?"

Marcia again turned back to Jennifer, the smile still on her face.

"I was getting milk out of the cooler." She paused. "There isn't much there, or on the shelves."

Jennifer's frustration with Marcia's distracted chatter finally made an impression on a hyped Marcia.

"Sorry. Anyway, I saw someone coming up behind me, they were reflected in the glass. It was Elizabeth. Blond hair, glasses, I could tell right away. She was yelling and shrieking at me."

She stopped speaking and turned back to look at what was going on. "There she is."

The two of them watched as the officers led a handcuffed, protesting Elizabeth out of the store and put her in the back seat of the cruiser. The quiet demeanour Elizabeth had presented at the funeral home had been replaced with a struggling, angry young woman. Marcia's smile was still plastered on her face. Jennifer's mouth still hung open in shock as the cruiser pulled away. They watched as the two military guys chatted briefly in the parking lot.

As the driver got in, he turned to Marcia.

"Not too shabby. I'm impressed." He and Marcia grinned happily at each other and high-fived. He looked at Jennifer, who was still trying to put the pieces together. "Ms. Elizabeth met her match in your friend here." He started the vehicle and they pulled away.

Marcia's phone beeped and she responded to the text. Jennifer sat back, shaking her head slightly, waiting for her to finish.

"Ryan will get the details when he gets home, it'll save me a trip to the station," Marcia said as she pocketed her phone. She turned back to Jennifer. "Where was I?"

"You decked her? I don't get it."

"Yeah." Marcia smile widened again. "Elizabeth came charging at me, all attitude and mouth. I'm taller and I was holding a three-litre bag of milk." She paused and scowled. "Shoot."

"What?" Jennifer was getting frustrated with Marcia's distractions.

"I forgot to get more milk. Anyway, Elizabeth took a swing at me so I slammed her with the milk bags I had just picked up."

"You sucker punched her with the milk bags, from the looks of it," came a voice from the front seat, followed by a deep chuckle.

"I was mad. It would be a frozen day in hell before I let that cold-hearted little monster get away with attacking me. Elizabeth dropped like a stone. I didn't mean to hit her *that* hard but she'd attacked me first, screaming that we had ruined her life. I just reacted." Marcia started to chuckle and the driver joined in. The atmosphere in the car was charged with a mixture of relief and laughter. Gone was the heaviness and grief of minutes ago.

"It was self-defence," Marcia added smugly.

The self-defence comment caused the driver to explode with laughter. Jennifer, even in her exhausted state, was not immune to their merriment. She felt laughter bubbling to the surface as she pictured the situation with the bag of milk, even if she didn't have all the details.

"That's my statement and I'm sticking to it," Marcia managed to squeak out. Looking over at her friend, Jennifer could see the tears running down Marcia's face as she and the driver continued to howl. Jennifer had a brief flashback to the day Captain Barry covered her with snow as she allowed herself the luxury of joining in.

"Two of the milk bags exploded when I hit her." Marcia managed to compose herself for a minute. "There was just enough of a tear in the outer bag to burst open and shower Elizabeth."

"Stop, make it stop," panted the driver. An adrenaline-fueled Marcia had no intention of stopping. She was on a roll. *Cold* was apparently her trigger word.

"She was out cold, showered with cold milk, lying on a cold floor!" Marcia, gasped for breath. "But not for long. She came to quickly, gave me a cold stare, staggered to her feet and tried to attack me again."

"I'm going to give both of you the cold shoulder if you don't stop using the word cold," Jennifer said, no longer immune to the merriment. It was a lost cause. There was no rhyme or reason for the laughter, other than too much sadness and exhaustion, and relief that the situation had not been more serious. It didn't matter. Elizabeth was in custody for attacking Marcia and Jeff and no one else was hurt.

"Bundle up," the driver said, as he dropped Jennifer off. "It's *k—k—kooold* out." As he pulled away, the muffled sound of the laughter faded into the night as the car pulled away.

Jennifer continued to smile as she walked to her apartment. She had no energy to climb under her own steam as she hauled herself up step by step with the railing. She dropped her portfolio by the door. Elaine's file had not been touched, there hadn't been time. The brief respite of merriment fled as she thought about Elaine, and then Victoria's sad face flashed through her mind. Her chest clenched and for the first time she begged God to put an end to her emptiness. There was no comfort to be had, no sense that she had been heard.

Mindlessly she fed and watered Grimsby and made herself a bowl of soup, dropping the dishes into the sink when she finished. She undressed and climbed into bed, her phone forgotten in her pocket. She was too tired to check her messages. It didn't even cross her mind as she fell into a dreamless sleep, Grimsby at her feet.

Morning seemed to come seconds after Jennifer lay down. Dragging herself out of bed, she ran her fingers through her hair, brushed her teeth and put on yesterday's clothes. Yawning, she gave Grimsby fresh water, picked up her portfolio and went downstairs to her office. Elaine's funeral was tomorrow and she needed to prepare. Once she was satisfied the details were covered, she scanned her emails.

Her shoulder slumped at the number of cancellations by funeral directors—sick or unable to do their shifts at the arena. She placed calls to recruit replacements, many going to voicemail as directors, too exhausted to answer, ignored their phones until they were ready to take calls. She scanned the report the temporary Transfer Coordinator, Lucas, had sent her, realizing he, too, was stretched for staff.

She sat back in her chair and closed her eyes for a minute before she rose to open the funeral home for the day. There was no sign of Roger yet. She looked down the street and didn't see him coming. She noted with surprise the snow that had blanketed them a few days ago (or was it weeks ago?) had receded. A van pulled in, the driver waved. It was John, from Blooms. She met him at the garage door.

"John!" she exclaimed as he entered. "You're hurt."

His mouth curved into a wry smile as he touched a bandage near his swollen eye.

"My fault. I should have kept the shop closed. But no, I got a small shipment in and I wanted to sell some of the fresh flowers."

Jennifer looked at him quizzically. A flower shop was a non-essential service. John had been servicing clients such as funeral homes by phone only.

"You know the gerbera farm in the western part of the region? They've been relatively untouched by the pandemic. They asked if I wanted a shipment of gerberas and I couldn't say no. They're one of my favourites. I felt the need to have the shop smell and feel like it used to. So, I had them deliver a load." He set down a large bouquet composed entirely of gerbera's and baby's breath on the shelf in the garage.

"These are for Elaine's funeral," he said sadly. "I wanted her to have something bright and pretty. It just won't be the same around here without her."

"No, it won't." The two of them paused to look at the bright, happy bouquet.

"Anyway, I opened the shop for a couple of days. A group of guys came in and demanded money. When they started trashing the shop, tossing plants and flowers around, I lost it—which is how I got the black eye. Served me right. The advisory to store owners was still in effect. I am a non-essential service."

"Except today," Jennifer responded softly as she touched one of the bright red gerberas gently. Elaine loved gerberas." She looked up at John, her eyes brimming with tears. "You knew that, didn't you?"

He nodded. "I have a couple of more arrangements in the back of the van. I imagine you could all use a bit of joy." He made several trips back and forth, until the shelf was lined with colour and scent.

"Oh, look!" John and Jennifer turned to see Marcia and Ryan entering the garage. "Their gorgeous!"

"They do brighten up the place," agreed Ryan as he and John greeted each other. "How's the eye?"

"Much better."

"Can you join us for coffee?" Jennifer asked.

"A quick one," John's said. "I know you don't have much time."

Marcia led him into the lounge as Ryan turned to Jennifer. "Just an update," he said. "You probably realize certain members of the population are in more jeopardy from influenza than the rest of us."

She nodded. She had a feeling he was talking about prisons. With tight quarters, staff shortages and lockdowns, convicts were trapped. If one guard brought in the flu, it had the potential to wipe out much of the prison population. The same was true of nursing homes. Vulnerable older people had little defense.

"While I have no specific word on Travis, I heard from a colleague the prison where he's incarcerated has a death rate from the flu at ten percent. There's been rioting. The guards are edgy and they have limited military support. If and when a list of deaths is released, I'll let you know.

"If Travis doesn't make it, there won't be a trial. I won't have to testify."

"Exactly."

Jennifer looked at Ryan thoughtfully. She'd been dreading the trial. Travis, the interim funeral director who covered the funeral home after Uncle Bill died, was a crime boss whose hatred of her for exposing him knew no limits. If he succumbed to the flu, she'd be free of his influence outside the prison. Deep down, she wouldn't be too sorry to see him gone. She needed to feel safe again.

"Jim called me," said Ryan, raising an eyebrow.

Jennifer's heart leapt. "Did they find Victoria?"

"You didn't call me," Ryan accused. "I would have put someone right on it. Sue has too much on her plate to chase down a suspected missing person. Mr. Patterson did call to report Victoria missing, but we had no available staff to pursue it. I checked the notes, Victoria went to the store to pick up something and didn't return. To answer your question, no, they have not found Victoria yet. They did find her car. Jim notified me."

Ryan's mild rebuke about not calling him was the least of her concerns.

"Where?"

"Northwest. At this point Jim has no idea where Victoria might be. Her cell phone hasn't been used since she disappeared. The provincial police are processing the car for prints and evidence."

Jennifer felt her shoulders slump and her energy drain. Ryan, sensed her concern. "Maybe she needed to get away for a while. From what Marcia told me, Victoria has suffered tremendous loss. It would be more than anyone could bear."

Jennifer raised her head and looked at Ryan, her misery reflecting in her eyes. "Or not. Someone may have wanted to harm her. You didn't see her kitchen. Even distraught, people don't—it doesn't matter. It might be too late. Why didn't I pay more attention, I should have supported her more."

"As Jim would say—should have, could have, the tyranny of the *oughts*," Ryan responded. "Let John's team and ours take care of finding Victoria. You and Marcia need to concentrate on getting enough rest and taking care of yourselves."

It was Jennifer's turn to raise an eyebrow. "You should talk."

"There *is* an end in sight. This pandemic has tested us past our limits. Too many deaths." He shook his head sadly.

"I'm glad you and Marcia can get away this weekend," she said brightly in an attempt to lighten the mood.

"I am looking forward to the weekend. Marcia and I both need some rest." He looked at her and scowled. "So do you." He squinted at her and cocked his head slightly to the side. "You've lost weight and you look exhausted."

"I'm doing my best to stay healthy," she responded. He looked at her cynically. She knew he didn't believe her, but he let it go.

Joining John and Marcia in the lounge, Jennifer made a coffee and sat. They were talking about Elaine's influence in the community and she listened with a heavy heart. She barely noticed Laura enter to tell her she had' a call from Mr. Whitney, the cemetery manager. Pushing herself out of the chair Jennifer went to her office and picked up the line.

"Hello," she said as pleasantly as she could. Even talking took more energy than she felt like expending.

"I'm so sorry to hear about Elaine," Mr. Whitney said. "I wanted to call you personally to express my condolences and to tell you we are now able to proceed with burials. With the snow almost gone, we'll have the gravesite ready for tomorrow."

"That's very kind of you. Thank you."

"You're welcome, Ms. Spencer."

After placing the receiver in the phone cradle, she sat back in her chair and closed her eyes, feeling the sting of tears behind her lids. Her heart ached with loss.

A tap on her door broke into her grief, it was Laura again, this time with a list of messages. One was from Roger from the night before, saying he would be late. *At least he's OK.* She had come to depend on him to keep the funeral home running.

Rather than deal with the list of calls, she rejoined Marcia and Ryan. Sitting down again, she stared into her mug. John was gone.

"Jennifer?"

She looked up at Ryan. His face showed his empathy.

"I have something I'd like to run by you."

She nodded her approval, somewhat distracted by John's kindness and her thoughts about Elaine's upcoming funeral service.

"What colour was Stephanie's hair when you first met her?"

"I dunno, black I think."

"What colour was Elizabeth's hair when you met her?"

"Blonde."

Ryan pulled a photo from his pocket and handed it to her.

"Look closely," Marcia said. Ryan shot her a "don't interfere" look and Marcia complied, fighting back a smile.

"That's Stephanie, she has black hair," Jennifer responded.

Ryan nodded. "Now look at this tattoo, do you recognize it?"

He handed her a photo of Stephanie's arm, a black tattoo of a zombie clearly visible. Ryan placed his hand over part of the tattoo photo, leaving the lower section exposed.

"Does that look like the tattoo you saw the night Jeff was attacked?"

She studied it carefully. "It does. In fact, it looks quite familiar."

"Think back to the day you went into Williams Funeral Home with Dimitri's wife. Althea?" He glanced at Marcia, who nodded her confirmation. "Do you remember the sketch you and Marcia pulled from the garbage? The one Althea threw out?"

Staring at the photo, she did her best to recall the details. The tattoo appeared to be a match. She closed her eyes to visualize the day Marcia confronted Stephanie. Marcia, tall and slender at 5'7" was a good four or five inches taller.

"Elizabeth is Stephanie?" Incredulous, she looked over at Marcia.

Marcia nodded. "Ryan talked to me about it last night and I saw the photos this morning. Drew's mom told me he had a tattoo removed after he lost his license. It was a painful process for him, and it left a large scar. When Drew and Stephanie were together, both got the zombie tattoo, the one Stephanie had drawn. Ryan will call Drew's mom to ask what kind of tattoo Drew had to confirm it, but I think they're a match. Drew's scar was the right size."

Exhaling, Jennifer sat back in her chair, looking first at Ryan, then back to Marcia.

"That shriek, the day she pushed Jeff onto the ice, how could I have not recognized it was Stephanie?" Her Elizabeth persona was a far cry from her "Stephanie" personality. A wave of remorse swept over her, threatening to overwhelm her with guilt. "If I'd had been paying attention, Jeff might not have been attacked."

"Don't beat yourself up," Ryan said. "You only met Stephanie a few times. Judging from what Sue told me, Stephanie is a master manipulator. Blonde hair, glasses, the demur demeanor, makeup that made her look less gaunt. She blended into her environment well as Elizabeth. She was quite convincing when she made her statement last night. She didn't attack Marcia, Marcia attacked her. She insisted Jeff had threatened her too, and that Drew was abusive."

A tiny smile played around Marcia's lips. "It *was* self-defence."

Ryan's lip twitched as he tried not to betray his amusement. Obviously, he and Marcia had discussed the events of the night before and had shared a laugh.

"It's the other way around," he said to his wife dryly as their eyes met, communicating as only couples do.

"Why did she get a job here? It doesn't make sense." Jennifer leaned forward. "We fired her, she had no skills, no insight."

"It makes sense if you understand how she thinks," Ryan said. "Stephanie is obsessed with death and death paraphernalia. She has a casket tattoo on her leg, a tombstone on her shoulder and the zombie on her forearm. However, the real-world job of dealing with death and grief overwhelmed her. It did not meet her expectations or support her fantasy."

"She's a death groupie," Marcia said pragmatically.

Jennifer looked from Marcia to Ryan, flabbergasted.

"You notice she seldom spoke, that she let Jeff speak for her? Had she talked more, we might have picked up that Elizabeth was Stephanie. She *knew* that, which is why she avoided us," Marcia added.

"Elizabeth is Stephanie's middle name," Ryan added. "She was extremely angry with Drew for removing the tattoo. Even after she left him, which was the day after you girls fired them, she continued to text and call him. He didn't respond to her and that's why she wanted him dead."

Tucking the photo into his pocket, Ryan rose. "Thanks Jennifer." Leaning over to give his wife a peck on the cheek, he left to go to work. Marcia's eyes followed him out of the room.

"Ryan has accepted the position of Lieutenant. It's a big change for him. I'm glad we're going away this weekend. His job places a lot of demands on him. We have to snatch every minute we can together," Marcia said, almost sadly.

Jennifer looked at her friend closely. "Your job is intense and demanding too." Squaring her shoulders and sitting up, she added brightly, "Don't forget, you still have your honeymoon trip to look forward to." She tried not to think ahead, if the pandemic swept through in its second wave, the trip might not happen.

As Roger entered the lounge, she left to call the driver to go the arena. Marcia would be taking care of the details of Elaine's funeral. Jennifer had a shift to do at the arena before she started work on registration.

Her thoughts strayed back to Victoria and the last time they talked at the grocery store. She couldn't recall if someone had been nearby, listening in on their conversation but she hadn't seen Victoria get into her car that day. Maybe if she'd paid attention.... Jennifer slammed her hand on the door frame, her frustration threatening to overwhelm her. *I can't do this anymore, I just want it all to go away. I need to be alone.*

The driver pulled up and she climbed into the vehicle, feeling bereft and helpless. *The pain is not going to go away, it's just going to get worse.*

13

Over coffee the next morning, Marcia and Jennifer reviewed the day's agenda, starting with Elaine's funeral.

"Would you like to drive lead or coach?" she asked Marcia.

"Coach. That is, if you're OK with driving the lead car."

"I'd prefer not to drive coach, not this time." Before Marcia could respond, Roger entered the lounge, a solemn reminder to both women Elaine's funeral was a few hours away. He greeted them pleasantly.

"I'd better get moving, I still have to go to the arena before the funeral." Rising, Jennifer went into her office, all other thoughts gone. Staffing the arena was her first priority, regardless the myriad of other concerns vying for attention in her head.

As she scanned the list of cancellations for the arena staffing, her shoulder's slumped. Picking up the phone, she started making calls. It took almost an hour to staff the arena for the day and evening. She decided to call the directors who would be in the following day, doing her best to be proactive. For the two that were unable to make their shift, she asked each of them to find their own replacement. She just didn't have the energy or time to do it for them. Neither man objected, they had heard about Elaine's death and knew her funeral was foremost on Jennifer's mind.

Standing up, she stretched and yawned and opened the door to the workroom to see Lucas at the computer.

"How's it going?" she asked.

"I'm trying to hire more people," he said. "Can you do a training session this afternoon? I've managed to locate a couple of students."

"Can't this afternoon. Any chance they could come in early this evening?"

Lucas nodded slowly and looked up at her, fatigue etched in his young face. "Oh, right, I'm sorry. It's your office manager's funeral today. I'll do my best. Do you have any idea when Jeff is coming back?"

"No, I haven't heard from his mom for a few days. When did you last speak with him?"

"The day after he got the flu, haven't heard from him since." He ran his fingers through his sandy blond hair and let out a deep sigh. "I'll get back to you about the training. I'm going to ask Brad to help me out. I need a few days off."

"Who's Brad?"

"He's a music student at university. He was hired a few weeks ago and I could use some help. He's the most likely choice."

Jennifer had done too many training sessions to even remember who was who. Brad was just another face in the crowd and she had no memory of him. She had to leave the transfer team in Lucas' hands, she had enough on her plate.

"Thanks. I'll make sure the arena staff get the details when you text me."

Checking the time, she walked back into her office and picked up the phone. Captain Barry answered on the second ring.

"I'll be over shortly to pick you up. The driver is out and we need you here on registration."

After they disconnected, Jennifer went into the lounge and leaning up against the counter, groaning audibly. She hated doing the death registration. Walking among the rows and rows of bodies in the cold seemed to freeze more than just her body. A piece of her soul numbed each time she did a shift. It was a horrific task. The cries of the families pierced her heart as they looked for their children, their parents or siblings. She had to step over body after body to find people and ensure the documentation was correct. More than once she'd stepped on a limb or stumbled over a body bag. There was no dignity for the unfortunate victims. They were becoming mere bodies to her now, numbered white bags on the ice. It was just like Chaplain Clive said it would be.

Jennifer longed for the luxury of a long bubble bath, a walk at the falls or a chance to sleep in. She'd felt herself change as the pandemic progressed and the changes sucked the life out of her.

Roger entered the lounge with a pleasant, "hello again" and she snapped out of her reverie to respond. If he was exhausted, he didn't show it.

"Is Marcia here? I have to see a family and there's another coming in shortly."

"I believe so. Laura would know for sure." Pushing herself away from the counter she went out the garage door to wait for Captain Barry. With the snow gone, the breeze carried a hint of spring. She inhaled deeply, wanting to keep the freshness with her, hoping it would cleanse her inside and out. She was tired of the scent of death, tired of the arena, tired of the workload and the pandemic.

She leaned up against the building, listening to the birds, aware it was the only sound in a usually active neighbourhood. There were few cars out, the gas shortage limited driving. People were not leaving their homes, children did not play outside with their friends, everyone was afraid to be around others who might pass on the flu. Few families had escaped illness or death. The silence was almost oppressive and she was relieved to hear Captain Barry's vehicle pull into the lot.

"Hello, Jennifer," he said cheerfully as she climbed into the jeep.

"Hi Captain, how are things?"

"Looking better. We may be able to get rid of one of the refrigerated trucks by the end of tomorrow. I was going over the stats today, the flu has peaked and we're now on the down side. I'd like to see the other arena closed by this time next week."

"That is a relief." That left one refrigerated truck plus the arena floor still full into next week. Her work was not done until the rink closed. The relief she should have felt at the news did not materialize.

"How many weeks has it been?"

He pondered his answer. "This is week ten, I think." She didn't respond, it was just small talk. She needed to focus on the tasks ahead.

"I'll have to leave for a couple of hours for Elaine's funeral. This evening I'll also be gone for a few hours to train transfer staff," she told him.

"Can you train at the arena?"

"I didn't think of it. I'll ask Lucas if he could arrange to have the trainees meet us there."

She pulled out her phone and called him while Captain Barry drove on.

"Sure Ms. Spencer. I haven't called them yet."

"Text me with the names, I'll leave the information with the front gate. Thanks Lucas."

Jennifer leaned her head back and closed her eyes. The drive to the arena no longer interested her; after last night's incident with Stephanie, it frightened her. The city seemed almost foreign now, it was desolate and deserted—shops boarded up and sidewalks empty. The exception was the occasional gang roaming around, looking for food and for people to rob. She wondered if the city would ever return to its previous vitality, if it would ever be the same.

Seconds later she felt the jeep slow. They were at the arena—she had dozed off. Shaking off the new wave of nausea from her brief nap, she thanked Captain Barry as she followed him in. The air inside assaulted her senses with the smell of death. She fought the bile rising in her throat.

Jennifer left her phone with the Sergeant at the desk, asking him to pass on the text with the names of the trainees to the front gate, and the funeral directors to the prep room supervisor when it chimed or rang, then went straight into the arena. She worked with the embalming teams for a while, showered and went to the ice. Ignoring the bodies, she walked, eyes forward, to the desk to begin the task of registering the dead.

The day held little meaning, just a series of tasks that had to be completed. Several times, she registered the death of people she was acquainted with: the principal at the high school, the young woman at the shoe store she and Marcia frequented. She did her best to ignore the feelings their deaths threatened to evoke.

She stopped long enough to eat and drink a bit, and check once more on the preparation room staff. An hour before Elaine's funeral, she had the driver take her home. She had processed dozens of bodies.

Scooting upstairs to her apartment after the driver dropped her off, she filled Grimsby's food and water dish. Too lazy to wash his regular bowls, she piled them in the sink along with the other dirty dishes and pulled clean dishes from the cupboard.

Her phone beeped constantly. She ignored the list of texts and emails. They could wait. She ran a brush through her hair and stared at her reflection in the mirror. She looked as bad as she felt, gaunt and tired. *Elaine always showed up for work immaculate and well-groomed. I can make the effort for her funeral.* Taking the extra few minutes to apply mascara and blush, she noted the change in her appearance and knew Elaine would approve.

Jennifer's throat tightened as she opened the apartment door to go downstairs. It would be a difficult afternoon.

Once downstairs, she could hear Brent, Roger and Marcia talking in the lounge. She hadn't seen Brent for over a week and greeted him first, plastering a smile on her face, which required more effort than she felt. Roger merely nodded when she greeted him.

"Laura has a message for you. She said it's important," Marcia said.

"OK."

"Coffee?" Brent asked.

"Please. I'll be right back."

She found Laura in the office working on the files. She looked up as Jennifer entered.

"Jeff's mom asked that you call her immediately. She said she tried to reach you last night, there was no answer."

A flash of guilt hit her. Her voicemail must have been full. The messages and calls needed attention and she had ignored them.

"Thanks. I'll be in my office."

She made her way back to the lounge, thanked Brent and, picking up her coffee went into her office and shut the door. Checking her phone, she noted the list of messages and calls. Two of them were from Jeff's mother. Jennifer called her first. No answer. Puzzled, she decided to try again after she'd completed the list. She'd barely started before there was a tap at her door. It was Roger.

"I think you need to come out here. Jeff's mother's here. Marcia nearly passed out and Brent is with them both now."

She heard Roger's words but they didn't register right away. *Marcia almost fainting?* That wasn't like her. She rose to check on her friend.

Brent had his arm around a sobbing Marcia. Jeff's mother was in the chair beside her, the two women holding hands. Brent's face said it all as he looked up.

"No. Please God, no!"

Brent nodded at her, his face awash with grief.

"No! Not Jeff. No, no, no." A strangled moan rose from deep inside her.

Focussing on Jeff's mother, she covered the space to her in a few steps. The sobbing woman clung to her, rocking back and forth. Rage, hot and quick, boiled and rose from the bottom of her soul. First Elaine, now Jeff. She abruptly pulled away from Jeff's mom and went into her office. Pulling out her phone, she texted Ryan, shaking with rage.

"Stephanie killed Jeff. He's dead." She slammed her finger on the send icon, trembling with a level of anger she hadn't felt in years. She knew she was out of control and chose not to go back to the lounge right away. She didn't trust herself to speak to anyone.

Minutes passed, her ragged breathing the only sound. Glancing at her computer, she noted the time. Elaine's funeral was to start in less than half an hour. She had to pull it together.

When she entered the lounge again, Brent and Jeff's mom were gone. Roger wasn't there either. Marcia and Sandy sat talking. She greeted Sandy quietly, before excusing herself on the pretext of checking to see if the minister had arrived. She hadn't been to the chapel yet to check on the set up, or to see if the flowers were in place. She hadn't taken the time to spend a few minutes alone with Elaine either. Not one part of her morning routine pre-funeral checks had happened, the time had slipped away. She hadn't done her job.

Still shaking, Jennifer's anger roiled at Jeff's unnecessary death. Her mind refused to focus on the details of Elaine's funeral—she felt detached from it all.

She found Roger in the lobby speaking with some people she didn't recognize. She went into the front office to ask Laura if the minister had arrived.

"Not yet," came the response. Laura had barely answered when Jennifer heard the front door opened and turned to see if it was the minister. It was Mr. Whitney, the cemetery manager. She went into the lobby to greet him.

"I hope you don't mind, Ms. Spencer. Elaine and I go way back, she was a year behind me in school. I dated her a few times. I'll just take a seat in the chapel." He walked past her and she watched as he picked up the pen, signed the register, and slipped into the chapel.

A breathless minister broke her reverie as he entered the funeral home.

"Sorry, Ms. Spencer. I'm running late. Is Sandy here?"

"No problem, this way." He followed her to the lounge, removing his coat as they walked. "I'll hang it up for you," she said, taking it from the minister.

She watched as the two men hugged, anxiety tightening her chest. She couldn't bear the thought of burying Elaine. She hung up the clergyman's coat and went to her office, standing with her back on the door, staring ahead at nothing in particular. She took some deep breaths before she left again.

Walking to the back of the chapel, Jennifer was surprised to see it almost full. Laura had been greeting people and directing them. She could see Desta sitting in the middle row with Peter and Jordan and Brent.

Marcia and the minister came up beside her and led her to the side door of the chapel. Marcia nodded to the minister and together they followed him, wheeling Elaine's casket to the front, stopping between the gerbera arrangements. Jennifer followed Marcia in a daze down the aisle to join her staff for the service. The minister talked about Elaine's impact on the community, her kindness, her commitment to helping others. Jennifer barely heard him.

As the minister closed the service, Desta succumbed to a small burst of sobbing. Squeezing her eyes shut. Jennifer made no effort to stem the flow of tears escaping her tightly closed lids.

At the final amen, the staff rose. Peter and Jordan wheeled the casket to the coach as Jennifer opened the chapel doors, and the coach door. Brent moved in to instruct the pallbearers and Marcia led the minister to the lead car as Jennifer took Sandy, who'd taken Desta's arm, to the family car. She watched Mr. Whitney climb into his vehicle and pull out of the lot, going ahead of them to the cemetery to ensure everything was in place. Brent let her know he would be going back to Williams Funeral Home to meet with Jeff's mom. She had decided to have his service there.

Jennifer scanned the small row of vehicles before climbing into the lead car. This time she had no anxiety about leading the procession. She was too numb with grief to even think about being afraid of losing her way. The whole day she felt as if she was outside herself. As she drove Elaine to her final resting place, her tears continued to flow unchecked down her cheeks. The minister did not speak, he sat in silent support beside her as they drove.

Mr. Whitney stood a respectful distance from the grave when they pulled up. As Jennifer exited the lead car, he walked over, opened the door for the minister, then tucked her arm in his and led her to Elaine's grave to check the set up. It was immaculate.

She did not let go of his arm, letting her staff take care of the details. As the minister started the service, she broke down completely, sobbing as if her heart would break. It was Mr. Whitney who stood tall and strong beside her, who took the committal sand from her trembling hands and made the sign of a cross as the minister uttered his final words of "earth to earth, ashes to ashes, dust to dust." It was Mr. Whitney who steered her to Sandy, who clung to her tightly.

"I miss her so," she said.

"I can't imagine life without her. It's too much to process," he responded as he pulled away and walked with Marcia and Peter to the family car.

Mr. Whitney, still supporting her, waited beside the grave until the mourners had left.

"I'll drive the minister home for you, Jennifer. You've been through enough." Walking her to the car, Mr. Whitney opened the door for her. Only then did he let go of her arm. Looking at his tired face, she could see the sympathy reflected in his eyes. Standing on her toes, she placed her hands on his shoulders and leaning forward, kissed his cheek softly. Wordless, she turned, climbed into the lead car and drove to the funeral home, full-blown sobs erupting anew as she cleared the cemetery gates.

Sitting in the parking lot of the funeral home, Jennifer called the military driver to pick her up to go to the arena. She didn't want to go into her funeral home. She didn't want to talk to her staff.

She scanned her phone. Brent had texted her to say he'd completed the arrangements with Jeff's mom. The funeral was scheduled for the next morning. It would be a small service with just staff and his mom and a few of his friends. Jennifer set the time of the service on her phone to alert her.

When the driver came for her, she said nothing on the way to the arena. She spoke with a few families there, still feeling as if she was detached from her body.

Jennifer completed the training session later in the day with Lucas. It was just work, rote and meaningless and it was after midnight before she asked to be taken home. It was the worst day of her life.

Entering Williams Funeral Home the next morning, the first person Jennifer sought out was Desta. Desta's beautiful face was streaked with tears and as their gazes met. Jennifer hugged her firmly. She saw Brent speaking quietly with Marcia and Jeff's mom and she led Desta across the lobby to speak with them. Jeff's mother looked as if she'd aged overnight, her grief draining her of her life's essence and energy.

"I almost forgot," Jeff's mom said, her voice flat as she reached into her purse, pulling her hand out gently. She looked at Marcia. "I found Buddy on the bottom of his cage this morning." She handed Marcia a small bundle wrapped in paper towel. "Can Buddy go with Jeff? He loved that bird so."

Simultaneously Brent steadied Marcia, who accepted the budgie in her outstretched hand. Marcia's face was void of colour. Jennifer instinctively moved to Jeff's mom, who broke down as she released the budgie to Marcia's care, her wracking sobs surrounding the little group with renewed pain. Jennifer watched as Marcia tenderly pulled the little bird to her chest. She heard Desta's sobs and the sound of her own crying and observed Brent's tear-streaked cheeks. It was the worst week they had faced as they shared the loss of their second colleague.

This is my family. Two losses are too much to carry. Victoria has been through it too. I have to check with Jim, no one should bear that kind of pain, ever. I promise you Victoria, someone will find you.

14

Five days had passed since Elaine's funeral and Jeff's service. Jennifer barely noticed the time slip away. She didn't care if she ate, her sleep was plagued with dreams of rows of bodies and shadows lurking and of sadness and death.

She went through the motions of caring for Grimsby, barely connecting with him when he settled in her arms, purring. She ignored her appearance, meeting what she considered minimum standards: hair combed, body showered, clothes clean. The air was warm with spring; she barely noticed. She had kept her promise to Victoria and called Jim, he was vague about details, saying only that they were no closer to finding her. Jennifer had given up all hope of them finding Victoria alive. But then, something twigged at the very back of her mind.

"The last time I saw her was at the grocery store. Later that month when Marcia and I stopped by the corner store to pick up milk"—and a crazed/deranged Stephanie—"I saw something in the shadows. I didn't clue in at first, but it was people."

"Probably a gang waiting to see if they could jump you."

"Yes, exactly. Like what happened when I drove the Lieutenant's wife over to Williams' to see a casket."

"OK, but I'm not following you. We've suspected the gangs from the start but we haven't—"

"—gotten anywhere. I know. But, when I visited Victoria's house it was clear she'd been in the middle of baking again. Like the last time we spoke. Maybe there's a gang that frequents the alley by the grocery store, just like the one that hovered in the shadows of the corner store. What if you caught one of the members and…" She didn't want to say what was actually on the tip of her tongue—*beat* the information out of him.

"You may be onto something there, Jen. Thanks. I'll let you know if anything pans out."

"Yeah. Thanks, Jim."

Maybe there'd been a reason for the dark, moving shadows in her nightmares after all.

The day the arena closed, Jennifer supervised the moving of the equipment in the preparation room back to its rightful owners. Roger had announced a few days before that he was finished, the funeral home no longer needed him. Jennifer asked Desta to ensure he was given a bonus with his last pay cheque. She shook his hand at the completion of his final day, a signal to her the pandemic was over (for now) and an acknowledgement to him she respected him and appreciated his work.

Marcia insisted she take some time off. Jennifer agreed to go away for a few days. She hadn't talked to John in weeks. Any updates about Victoria came via Jim, few though they were and never promising. It didn't matter. They were both too busy anyway, and she had nothing left in her to give.

As the final truck pulled away from the arena, Captain Barry suggested he walk her to her car, which she'd driven only once in the weeks of the pandemic, the day she drove lead for Elaine's funeral.

"We processed almost eighteen thousand bodies though here," he said as they walked outside toward her car. "That's about five percent of the population of this region."

She looked at him dully. The statistics meant little to her.

"This is just the first wave. If the second one is more virulent, which it may be, it's going to be a bigger challenge. At least we have time to prepare."

"Do we?" There was a bitter edge to her voice.

"Theoretically, yes. Practically, we could have used more military in this sector. We were stretched too thin."

"So was the bereavement care sector, so was the health care sector, so were the police." Aware of the bitter tone of her voice, she softened it. "Will you be back?

He looked down at her, his care-worn face kind.

"This has affected me in ways I didn't think possible. I've changed." They'd reached her car and he leaned up against it, folding his arms. She stood slightly right of him, watching the expression on his face, listening intensely.

"As a career officer I was in charge of large groups of men. Now I'm not even in charge of myself." He stared straight ahead, his eyes welling with tears as he spoke those words. In spite of her exhaustion and her own pain, she wanted to wrap him in her arms to comfort him. Instead, she remained silent, waiting.

He rubbed his eyes with his left hand and pulled a linen handkerchief from his pocket, blowing his nose gently.

"I had a meeting with my staff. Not one of us has been unscathed by this event. I encouraged them to seek help, to bond again with their families, take time for themselves. I was 'preaching' to myself with those words. The pandemic broke me." He folded his arms against his chest again, as if to protect himself from his next statement.

"So, to answer your question, no. I won't be back. I'm retiring. I need my wife and family." He pushed himself off the hood of the car and reached over to open Jennifer's car door.

"You and your team of funeral directors made an impact on my life. I'll never forget you. I see selflessness, a yearning to help others in you *and* your team. And you've lost weight, you know. You look exhausted and beaten down. It's time for you to take care of yourself again, too."

She didn't answer, just climbed into the driver's seat. "Goodbye, Captain. Thank you." She put her keys in the ignition and started the car.

"Goodbye, Ms. Spencer. It was a privilege working with you." He closed the car door, about-faced and with his back straight, his long stride took him back to the arena. He didn't look back.

Jennifer put the car in drive and went through the now-deserted gate. She too, did not look back. The horror of what the team had to do was behind her as she drove to the funeral home. Her report to the Public Health officials, with her recommendations, had to be compiled, *after* she surveyed the area funeral directors to get their input. *Once that's over, I'm finished. Like the Captain, like so many others. I am done in more ways than one.*

15

With the arena closed, the pace at the funeral home increased. Although the pandemic wound down, the hospital still needed the morgue cleared quickly in order to avoid overflow and cost increases. The hospital encouraged families to contact a funeral home immediately when a death occurred.

Marcia left for another weekend away with Ryan, leaving Jennifer and Peter and Laura. The pace was steady and Jennifer asked Brent to send his new employee, Brad, on all her transfers, too.

Bradley was short and stalky, an easy-going young man in his late twenties. He had lost his job when the auto shop he worked at was forced to close when the flu claimed the life of the owner. His laid-back demeanour hid a strong work ethic. Brent was happy to have him. With a shortage of workers, hiring remained a problem.

Marcia returned from her weekend pensive and quiet. She and Ryan had gone up north to a lake. The area was deserted, the small towns had been decimated. "They were like ghost towns," she'd told Jennifer. "It was as if all the people had vanished."

Ryan contacted her a few days after he returned to tell her Travis had survived the pandemic. He also explained the trial would be delayed indefinitely until the courts were staffed and caught up. It was not what Jennifer wanted to hear. She had enough trouble sleeping, eating and pushing through the stress and fatigue as it was.

The supply chains for gas and food and supplies were slowly opening up. Schools were to remain closed, with the intent of opening again in September. Colleges and universities were offering limited classes and Peter would be returning to school for a two-week consolidation before starting his apprenticeship. There was little in the news about the possibility of a second wave, although preparations were made by health care services and the military and government regardless.

People started going out more, greeting their neighbours in their yards, walking to the parks, enjoying the spring. Rain washed away the dust and dirt, adding to the potholes the work crews had been unable to repair during the pandemic.

Work was plentiful, from government jobs to doing people's yard work. Flu cases dwindled into the single digits as the pandemic slipped away as quietly as it had come in.

Jennifer still had not called her mom. It was two weeks after the arena closed before she sat down on her couch, Grimsby in her lap, and dialed her mom's number.

The line was busy, and she let out a sigh of relief. *At least I tried. I'll try again later this week.* She knew she was lying to herself, she'd put it off as long as possible. She was putting off a lot of things: her apartment needed cleaning, she needed a haircut, and she still had to compile the survey result for the Public Health department.

With a deep sigh, she picked up her laptop, pushing a complaining Grimsby off her knee. An hour and a half later her report to the Public Health Department was complete. Hitting send, she shut down her computer and rose, stiff and sore from the couch. It was nearly midnight and she hadn't eaten since lunch. She was checking her cupboards for non-existent snacks when her phone rang. It was Anne.

"Hi," she said, her voice dull and flat.

"You sound chipper," came Anne's dry response. "I know it's late, but I wanted to tell you mom called earlier tonight. I'll be going up tomorrow. I've finished here in Ottawa. Once I get back, I'll be moving to Toronto. I start my new job in two weeks.

"How long will you be with mom?"

"A few days. She wants me to help her get the estate settled. She hasn't changed the bank account or filed for her death benefit or even called the lawyer."

"Why is she so helpless?" Jennifer had little patience for her mom that late at night. A small part of her brain warned her she had little patience for her mom any time. She pushed the thought away.

"She is co-dependent," Anne said bluntly. "You know that. I'll help her get started and I'll come back. Hopefully, I'll get a chance to suggest she get help, but I suspect it'll fall on deaf ears. It's late. I'll talk to you in a few days."

"OK." Jennifer disconnected. *I don't care.* She flicked off the light, brushed her teeth, and fell into another night of restless, troubled sleep.

Several days later, when she and Maria were having coffee, Anne phoned again. Surprised that

Anne would call during the day, she answered it quickly.

"What's up?"

"Just wanted to let you know mom and I saw the lawyer, got the paperwork filed for the details relating to dad's death, and did the necessary banking. Once that was done, mom started running a fever. I was going to come home, but I think I'll wait until her fever drops. I'd feel better if I knew she was able to look after herself."

"How are you holding up?"

"Good. Other than making sure mom stays fed and hydrated, there isn't much to do. Jim and I have been on the phone a lot lately. I miss him. I can't wait to get to Toronto and settle in with him. How're you doing?"

Jennifer suppressed another one of the all too frequent sighs that seemed to escape her body before she answered.

"It's slowing down, we averaged two calls a day this week. More than a few are death by suicide, people just can't cope. Laura is still learning. It's hard without Elaine here." A sob erupted as she said those words and she caught herself. It did not escape Anne's attention. *Victoria is still missing. I've failed her.*

"You need some time off, and by time off, I mean away from the funeral home."

Composing herself, Jennifer did her best to make her voice light. "Vegas. I'd love to go to Vegas."

"Me too," Anne said wistfully. "We always have such a good time. Even if it was for a few days, I'd love to go. Maybe once I settle into my new job and can get away, we'll go."

"Sounds like a plan. I have to run, Marcia's flagging me down. Catch you later."

"Bye for now."

Marcia looked at Jennifer intensely. "I did not flag you down." Jennifer shrugged. "Sit," Marcia commanded.

Jennifer sat, feeling a bit guilty at being caught in a lie.

"When *are* you going to take some time off? Brent did, I did, the rest of the staff has paced themselves, taken days off and looked after themselves. What's stopping you?"

As always, Marcia could see right through her. This time it was annoying.

"Work."

"That's a pretty poor excuse if you ask me. You have staff, we can manage. You didn't answer my question, *work* isn't an answer."

Jennifer wanted to scream back at her friend, but she fought the urge. "I don't know."

"We promised each other, with our 'no holds barred' pact, we'd be honest. So, here it is, girlfriend. You need to get away. It's spring. Go to the cottage, go to the moon, do what you have to do. Just go."

"Yeah." Jennifer rose, picked up her phone and tucked in into her pocket. "Maybe later this week."

"Maybe?"

"Later this week. I'm going to the crematorium, need anything while I'm out?"

"No, we're caught up."

Without another word, Jennifer went to the garage, leaving Marcia sitting in the lounge. She was irritable and angry and sad and frustrated and tired.

Maybe Marcia was right, maybe she did need to get away. A few minutes later she admitted to herself that Marcia *was* right.

As she drove down the quiet highway she reflected on her mood swings, her inability to sleep, her apathy. *I don't want to go away. I don't want to stay here either. I can't stand my own company right now.*

She spent the next few days avoiding Marcia and her staff as much as possible. Anne called early one morning, three days after they last spoke.

"I don't know how to break this to you, so I'll just come out with it. Mom died last night. The doctor came here to pronounce her. The funeral home just picked her up." Anne used her old "just the facts" voice as she presented the news.

"Do you want to have a service? A committal?" Jennifer was aware she was completely detached from the personal impact the news should have had, and was in funeral director mode.

"I don't think so. You?"

"No." A long pause echoed over the line. Both sisters had stopped talking, the air between them heavy with the silence. "Are you OK?"

"I am. We can talk later about this. Jim and I have been on the phone half the night. I'll be going home tomorrow. He's been my support."

"That's good. Call me if you need me."

"Will do."

It was Anne's call that helped her make her decision to get away. She said nothing to Marcia or Brent. Jennifer went upstairs immediately and threw some things into a bag. She packed Grimsby's extra dishes and some food, before making herself a tea.

She went through the rest of her day as she had in past days, simply going through the motions. She waited until the next morning to call her twin again.

Anne, who usually depended on Jennifer to take care of details and deal with the emotional parts of family drama, had stepped up. Usually that task fell on a reluctant, but more patient, Jennifer. She picked up her phone and dialed Anne's number.

Her sister answered immediately, "Hi Jen." Not her usual greeting of "yes?"

"How's it going? How are you holding up?"

"It's rather odd. This town isn't the same as it was when we were growing up. It's so quiet. Businesses are closed, the streets are deserted, and there aren't many people left. The minister told me those who escaped influenza left to join family in other parts of the province, some around the country." When Jennifer didn't respond, Anne continued, sensing her sister needed to know the details.

"Mom didn't say much when I got here a few days ago. She didn't ask about you, she didn't ask what I'd been doing, just talked about dad and how much she needed him. The supermarket had closed, she was out of work. She'd aged so much since I saw her last. I was sleeping in the chair beside the bed when she died. She just, sort of, slipped away. I did manage to tell her the night before that she'd done her best raising us. It was the closest I got to telling her I loved her. I don't know if it was love, it was more of a choice I made not to let her die alone or let her feel she had failed us."

"She did fail us," Jennifer said bluntly. "I doubt she even cared. We were an inconvenience."

"I agree. And before I met Jim, I would have turned my back on her request to come and help. It was a bit of a shock to have her get sick so quickly after I arrived. Jim has helped me understand that love is more of a choice than a feeling. Haven't you said the same thing to me before? It never sank in. I listened to his version of why he thought mom was so challenging to be around, and I made the decision to just be there for her."

"We're adults now and we can put the past behind us. Unfortunately, I wish it had been different, that we grew up with support and love. I think I might have been less insecure and not so judgmental." Jennifer found herself surprised she and Anne were discussing the situation so calmly.

"Again, I agree. For me it was my avoidance of people. I buried myself in my work to forget the past. I saw myself as smarter than most."

"But you are smarter than most people. Your IQ is really high."

Anne gave a soft chuckle. "It's got nothing to do with my emotional IQ. Apparently, it's rather low. Jim has taught me I'm not just a brain, I need people in my life. I just didn't know it before, or rather I chose to ignore that part of me."

"Are you two going to marry?"

"Probably. We have a few months respite before the second wave of influenza hits, if it does."

"You didn't tell me much about your new job."

"Not much to tell. I'll be working in a newsroom as the assistant director for a national paper."

"Wow. Really? That's no small thing." For a brief second, Jennifer wondered why she hadn't shown an interest in Anne's move and her new job before now.

"It's no big thing, really," Anne said modestly, playing with Jennifer's words. "It's what I know and what I do and I love my work. Jim and I will be together, and I love that most of all."

Jennifer quietly pondered Anne's change of attitude and heart. She'd softened and matured and for her to look after their mother, let alone be with her, was a first.

"I'm glad you were there for mom, at least she didn't die alone. It's hard to believe she was only in her late forty's. I had hoped she'd pick up the pieces of her life and move on. Maybe she would have."

"I don't know," Anne responded thoughtfully. "Anyway, I'll be closing up the house today and going back to Ottawa. I've collected a few things for you, photos, school memorabilia, stuff like that. Is there anything else you want or need?"

"No, let the lawyer sell it off and sell the house. It probably won't go for much if the town doesn't recover from the pandemic."

"I expect not. All right, don't work too hard, you sound tired. I'll talk to you soon."

"Bye."

As Anne tapped off, Jennifer leaned back and closed her eyes. Her chest was heavy with anxiety and grief. She took a deep breath, forcing air into her lungs. She knew she should have taken some time off in the midst of it all. There were moments now she thought she was going to lose her mind. She was intrinsically weary and mentally and emotionally exhausted.

Reaching for the phone, she called Marcia downstairs rather than speak to her directly, to see if she would cover for the next few days. It was time for the "no holds barred" promise they'd made. She had to get away, it wasn't an option. She turned off her phone and waited until the afternoon visitation started before she slipped quietly out the garage door.

No one saw her leave. She didn't want them to.

16

Jennifer pulled into Anne's and her cottage driveway, barely noticing that the houses and cottages around her sat eerily quiet. There were no children playing, no cars parked outside the tidy little homes, no dogs barking, only a deep, empty silence broken by the occasional bird cheeping. The air was fresh and clean. She didn't care.

She picked up the few grocery bags she'd filled with what she'd found in her freezer and cupboard, grabbed her backpack and took everything inside, dumping the bags on the kitchen counter. Turning around, she went back out to the car and retrieved Grimsby, whose plaintive meowing indicated his unhappiness at being confined in his carrier.

"It's OK buddy, let's get you out of your prison and set up house," she said, placing his carrier on the floor and opening the door. He slowly emerged, stretching and yawning. He glanced around the unfamiliar surroundings and started his survey of the cottage.

Fifteen minutes later Jennifer had put the groceries away, turned on the water and gas and fed Grimsby. She had set up his litter box in the laundry room. The cottage was damp and cold, echoing the silence of the outdoors. She looked around at the decorating that Elaine and Sandy had done. Hugging her arms tight to her body, she walked to the screened-in front porch. Even the lake was still. It was as if time had stopped—like the lives claimed by the pandemic.

Jennifer wrapped a blanket around herself and stared out at the water, her mind unable to hold a thought or retrieve a memory. Darkness closed in, obscuring the water and the budding trees and still she sat, immobile. She wanted to scream just to hear the sound of something, of someone, even if it was just her voice alone.

Eventually, stiff and sore, she rose, made tea and nibbled on a few cookies. Food had no taste. She wasn't hungry. Food would not feed her empty heart and soul. She didn't care if she ever worked again, or spoke to anyone, or even smiled. She sighed, and the sound of her sigh seemed to trouble the air around her.

Jennifer pulled the covers back on the bed and lay down, too exhausted to brush her teeth or hair or put on pajamas. It was just a routine, it had no meaning to her now.

She slept fitfully, people flashing through her dreams asking for her help, crying out for their families. Victoria's sad face berating her that she hadn't kept her promise. Jennifer startled awake over and over, only to fall back into the same nightmares until the sun rose.

She stared at the ceiling for a long time before she had to get up to go to the bathroom.

Studying her reflection in the mirror for the first time in a while, she saw a shell of the woman she'd been staring back at her. She looked and felt like someone without a soul, no hope. Her sunken eyes were almost swallowed by dark circles; they did not sparkle or reflect the light. They too, were as vacant and as empty as she was. Her hair was dull and unkempt and still in need of a cut.

She made tea again, glanced at Grimsby's dishes and left the cottage, stopping only to put on her hoodie before wandering out into the early morning sun to the Muskoka chair on the shore.

Minutes, then hours, passed as she stared at the water. It was calm, no waves lapped the shore, they rolled in gently, not breaking as they reached the sand. Even the lake was silent—as silent as the hundreds of bodies that had been on the arena floor. *If I start walking forward and keep going until I can't keep going, it'll all stop. Just like it stopped for Elaine and Jeff and all the others. So many others, Victoria, Claire, her mom and dad.*

The sound of a car driving up penetrated her consciousness.

Go away. Leave me alone. She heard the dull thud of a door closing.

Just go, I don't want to talk to you, whoever you are. I don't want to talk to anyone ever again. She didn't turn around, she didn't care. Maybe if whoever it was knew she didn't care, they'd leave and not come back.

She remained motionless, unaware that the two people who had emerged from the car were talking quietly. One went into the cottage, she heard the screen door close, the other came up behind her silently.

"Jennifer."

Go away! the voice in her head screamed.

The voice of the lake, softer, enticed her, floating around the periphery of her consciousness.

There was a presence now, a sense that someone closed in on her. She closed her eyes and willed it to go away. The presence lingered, threatening to draw her to it.

"Jennifer." *I know that voice.*

She turned slightly. John stood a few feet away. For a second, his face reflected his shock at seeing her, but he recovered quickly.

"Come inside, you're shivering."

She shook her head no and turned back to the water. If she went inside, she might not get back out to the lake. It was calling her, and its voice promised peace.

The cottage door closed as the other person came out. Jennifer sensed John walk away from her. She vaguely heard a murmur as they talked. Maybe they were leaving. She wanted them gone.

Leave me alone. Please go. The lake was waiting. Its voice was stronger and more urgent.

A second presence closed in and before she could say a word, it scooped her up, strong arms enveloping her.

"No! Stop!" she shrieked, shattering the silence that had all but taken her soul.

"Jennifer, it's OK. It's me, Jim."

Jim. How could Jim be here? Shouldn't he be with Anne? How could he know she was desperately wanting to die?

"It's going to be all right, sweetie." He barely spoke above a whisper, his voice gentle, as if he knew her soul was close to shattering. "John's here. I'm here. We'll help you. You don't have to be strong anymore."

He carried her into the cottage, where a fire burned in the woodstove. He placed her gently on the couch as John wrapped a blanket around her.

"You're shivering." John's eyes showed concern. She hung her head and did her best to shut him out. She could hear Jim clattering around the kitchen.

"When did you eat last?" Jim asked as he handed a steaming cup of hot chocolate to John.

It took too much energy to shrug or shake her head. She didn't move.

"I thought so. John and I wanted you to know we found Victoria.

"*Victoria?* You found her? How?"

A gang of young homeless kids kidnapped her, they stole her groceries and car. They kept her in their hideout, forcing her to cook and clean for them while they tried to get a ransom. The female gang leader negotiated with her father who'd agreed to pay. But when the gang leader went to the drop off point, there was no money. Her father was too sick to get to the bank and too scared to call the police. His hospice worker had stopped coming because she was sick too."

Jennifer clenched her fist, she just wanted to hear if Victoria was going to be all right.

"Victoria couldn't access her parent's bank account. The house was locked up by the security team John sent and the gang could no longer pilfer the house. Prints found throughout the house led to the identification of some of the gang members. That helped us find the area where they were holding Victoria. It was harder to nail down the exact location. The gang dispersed at night, raiding and stealing. They were hard to pin down." He paused and took a deep breath. "But sometimes, there is justice. The gang leader succumbed to the flu. The gang started to fall apart and without their leader, they got sloppy. The police nabbed a few of them stealing from a convenience store and under interrogation, they caved. Jim picked up the pot of hot chocolate and poured a bit more in John's mug. Jennifer hadn't touched hers.

"Victoria is safe now. John has arranged for a counsellor to work with her for as long as she needs. She bonded with some of the younger gang members, they had suffered the loss of a parent or caregiver and looked up to her. She is a remarkable young woman.

I kept my promise. Jennifer tried to absorb the news.

"Once dinner's over, I'm going to Ottawa to help Anne move."

Anne. Her twin. She'd briefly forgotten about Anne. Anne would miss her if she let the lake take her, of course she would. Suddenly, Jennifer was desperately lonely for her twin and a tear spilled down her cheek. Anne would understand how hard it was. She could tell Anne about the pain, how empty and alone she felt. Anne would know the grief and deaths she'd witnessed had torn her soul and stolen her spirit. Anne would know how confused she was. Why had she not told her twin when they spoke earlier?

"Take a sip." John gently lifted her chin and put the cup to her lips. She complied and the warm chocolate slid down her throat. She took another sip, then another, the sweetness and warmth compelling her to continue. She wrapped her trembling hands around his on the mug and finished it, reveling in the simple pleasure.

He put the empty cup down and wrapped her in his arms, his strength and warmth enveloping her.

She felt safe. *No man is an island.* He'd said that to her at Christmas, before too many deaths, too many cold, still bodies had eroded the very essence of her being. She closed her eyes and felt and listened to his heart beating, and with each beat, a tiny part of her soul fluttered and revived.

Thank you for reading the Spencer Funeral Home Niagara Series. If you liked the book, please rate or review it—thanks!

You can find me on:
Twitter:
@richardsonjan1
Facebook:
Janice J. Richardson
Goodreads:
https://www.goodreads.com/author/show/14979647.Janice_J_Richardson

I would love to hear from you.

ABOUT THE AUTHOR

Jan Richardson was born in Toronto, Canada and has lived and worked in various parts of Ontario. Her original career choice was medical office assistant; her dream was to be a funeral director. Years passed, she fulfilled that dream and went to college, got her license and did a post-graduate certification.

She left funeral service to adopt and raise her special needs granddaughter, having raised a special needs daughter it was a natural progression.

Jan currently resides in the Niagara Region, and works as a personal assistant to her cat.